To everyone else, Megan appeared unflappable and unconcerned. She was in control, and there was nothing to worry about. As far as Ted and the boys and a few close friends knew, she was going in for some tests not because there was anything to worry about, but only as a sensible precaution. She was a nurse, after all, and knew about prevention. The word 'cancer' was never spoken, and perhaps no one but Megan even thought it. She gave the impression that the problem, if there was one, was simply a minor nuisance connected with the change of life. Certainly she looked healthy; rosy-cheeked, bright-eyed, as sturdy, efficient and cheerful as ever. Who would think to doubt her when Megan said that she was fine?

Also from Warner Books

CASUALTY:
SWINGS AND ROUNDABOUTS

# CASUALTY

# THE EARLY YEARS

## LAURA WARING

*From the television series created by
Jeremy Brock and Paul Unwin*

**WARNER BOOKS**

A *Warner* Book

First published in Great Britain in 1987 by Futura Publications
This edition published by Warner Books 1993

Copyright © Laura Waring 1987
Television Format and Series concept
© Jeremy Brock and Paul Unwin 1985

A CIP catalogue record for this book
is available from the British Library.

ISBN 0 7515 0664 8

Typeset by M Rules
Printed and bound in Great Britain by
Clays Ltd, St. Ives plc

Warner Books
A Division of
Little, Brown and Company (UK) Limited
165 Great Dover Street
London SE1 4YA

# Chapter One

Six o'clock: the night shift was nearly over. Tired though she was after a day and a night without sleep, for once Megan Roach wasn't looking forward to going home. She would rather keep busy – coping with other people's problems left her no time to brood about her own.

It had been a fairly quiet night in Casualty, and the patients were few; one overdose, one broken wrist, one suspected food-poisoning, and a couple of homeless alcoholics wanting shelter from the cold and wet.

As she passed through the waiting area, Megan saw that someone new had come in, a woman in a light-coloured raincoat, standing at the reception desk, leaning against it, rather, as she gave her details to Susie.

Megan abandoned the idea of a cup of tea in the staffroom, caught Susie's eye and gave her a nod to say that she would take over. Her step grew firmer, and her tiredness suddenly vanished before the need to be efficient.

'You're in luck,' said Susie to the woman. 'Here's a

nurse now. No need to queue tonight!' Then, to Megan, 'Cubicle two should be free.'

'Come along, love,' said Megan. 'What seems to be the trouble?'

The woman turned. She was about thirty, with brown hair, blue eyes and a round, Irish face – a face that would have been pretty if it had been less pale and strained. There was nothing particularly remarkable about her – Susie, at least, had seen nothing remarkable – but Megan's eyes widened, and she stared as if seeing a ghost. The arm she had raised to offer comfort or guidance to the patient now faltered and stopped short of touching the other woman, as if she didn't quite dare.

'Mam?' said Megan tremulously. 'Mam?' She was shaking all over.

Then, as Susie and the patient both watched in amazement, Megan's legs gave way beneath her, and she fell to the floor in a dead faint.

Megan knew something was wrong before she opened her eyes. When she opened them and saw the ceiling she *knew* something was wrong. That wasn't her bedroom ceiling. This wasn't her bedroom. This wasn't her bed.

Cautiously, she rolled her eyes first to one side and then the other, and saw the top of the yellow-green curtains that separated the cubicles in the casualty ward. Now she knew where she was, but not why.

2

She might doze off sitting bolt upright in the staff-room, but Megan – who had more than once ticked off other younger nurses for such unprofessional behaviour – would never stretch out for a nap while on duty, no matter how exhausted she might be, or how quiet the night.

She tried to sit up, but hands on her shoulders pushed her gently but firmly back.

Clive King was standing over her. 'Easy,' he said. 'Just take it nice and easy, Megan.'

'What's wrong?' she demanded. 'What's happened?'

'That's what we want to know.'

'What am I doing lying here? I'm not a patient.'

'For the moment, you are.'

'What? Why? What happened?'

'Susie say you fainted. She say you stare at that Mrs Mullan like she a ghost, and then you keel over.'

'Mrs Mullan . . .' Megan suddenly remembered that she was on duty, and tried to sit up. 'Where is she? I should be looking after her . . .'

Clive kept her down with an effortless use of his strength. 'You should be looking after yourself. Don't fret about Mrs Mullan; Duffy's with her now in one. Nothing wrong with her; cut herself trying to open a tin of catfood. Which wouldn't be so bad, if she'd cut herself on the tin, only she didn't; she cut herself on the opener. And she was using a knife because Puss was hungry and she couldn't take the

3

time to find a proper tin-opener.'

Clive's gentle voice and easy humour relaxed Megan. She stopped trying to sit up, and managed to smile back at him.

'Better,' he said approvingly.

The curtain opened, and Ewart Plimmer came in. 'How are we doing?' he asked.

'We're doing just fine, Ewart. At least, I am. Save your bedside manner for someone who'll appreciate it.'

'Thank you, Clive,' said Ewart, dismissing him with a look and a nod.

'Take it easy,' Clive said to Megan as he went out. 'Remember what I say: you got to take care of yourself before you can take care of other people.'

'All this fuss,' said Megan. She sat up, cautiously, and swung her legs around. 'I'm perfectly fine.'

'Are you?'

Megan paused, taking stock, and then nodded. 'Yes. Tired, but then it was nearly the end of the shift . . . a good day's sleep will put me right.'

Ewart shook his head. 'People don't faint because they're tired.'

'Ah, yes, I should have known I couldn't put one over on a medical man . . . tiredness is no excuse for fainting.' Her bantering tone suddenly faltered, and she could not meet his steady gaze.

'What was it, Megan? I saw Mrs Mullan; her wound was –'

'You think I'd faint at the sight of blood!' She stared at him, wide-eyed and indignant at this slur on her professional toughness. 'Did I faint when we had that carpenter feller in here wanting us to stitch his hand back on to his wrist? Did I faint when that Mr Brosnan began haemorrhaging and we were all splashing about in blood up to our ankles? Have I ever been too squeamish to do what needed to be done, in all the years we've known each other? Come on, Ewart! I'm no virgin.'

'So now we know why you *didn't* faint. Any thoughts about why you did?'

She wanted to brush aside his enquiries, to convince him that she was all right, that it had been a moment's weakness, not to be repeated, and certainly not worth fussing about. But Ewart Plimmer wasn't just another doctor, and he was more than merely her boss. They had known each other far too long to pretend otherwise. He wouldn't let her get away with a brush-off – and maybe she owed him something more.

Maybe she owed him the truth.

'You'll think I've gone mental,' she said. 'Maybe I have.'

Ewart waited.

Megan sighed, and gave him a straightforward look. 'If it was Duffy this happened to I'd say, well, what can you expect? Duffy with her astrology and premonitions and goodness knows what else, of course Duffy would see a ghost – Duffy would, but not me!'

'A ghost?'

'I know it sounds daft, but it's true. I don't believe in ghosts, but for a moment, I thought I was seeing one. That's why I fainted. When that woman – Mrs Mullan – when she turned round and I saw her I thought – only for a moment, mind you – I thought she was my mother. She was the very image of her. Even though I knew it couldn't be, knew it wasn't possible, the sight of her – shook me. To see someone you thought had gone forever . . . someone you *knew* was gone forever . . . suddenly, I wasn't sure of anything. I didn't know where I was. It was like I was a girl again, and she was still alive. I suppose that's why I fainted. I couldn't put together what I knew with what I saw, and so my mind took the easiest way out: curtains.' She clapped her hands together.

Ewart shook his head slowly, in wonder rather than disbelief. 'How long ago . . . how old were you when your mother died?'

'Twelve.'

'It must have been very difficult for you.'

'Oh, yes, and with three brothers and my father to look after . . . actually, I suppose that made it easier. I was so busy worrying about them, looking after them the way I knew my mother would have wanted, that I didn't have much time to be sorry for myself.'

'And you've gone right on doing that, haven't you? Looking after other people. Instead of yourself . . .'

'It's my job,' said Megan. 'I don't need looking after the way some people do. Now, please sir, may I go home? I promise not to faint again.'

'You're sure you're all right now?'

'Absolutely,' said Megan, lying through her teeth.

Still Ewart hesitated. Megan knew he wasn't satisfied, and she steeled herself to parry any further questions. But at that moment, with a clattering of curtain rings, Kuba Trzcinski entered.

'Megan! You are all right? I am worried, I am alarmed, I am so . . . so . . . despairing when I hear you are fainted!' He went down on one knee before her and clutched her hand.

Megan rolled her eyes.

'Well, seeing as you're in good hands,' said Ewart, ducking out.

'You are all right?' persisted Kuba. 'Speak to me, Megan! You do not know how I feel when they tell me you are fainted!'

'Oh, Kuba, don't make such a meal of it.'

'A meal? You want I should make you a meal? You are hungry? I am a good cook, you know, a very good cook –'

'No, I don't want you to make me a meal! That's just an expression. It means . . . it means I want you to let go my hand and stop fussing. It was only a little faint, nothing to be alarmed about – you can see, now, I'm perfectly all right.'

With a worried grimace the Polish porter peered into Megan's face, seemed to check her pulse, felt her cheek with the back of his hand, frowned harder. 'You are a little pale, no?'

'No,' said Megan firmly. 'I am not a little pale, I am fine, just tired of answering a lot of questions. There is nothing wrong with me, Kuba, nothing at all.'

As she left, Megan heard Kuba muttering, 'Make a meal. Make me a meal. Do not make me a meal . . . no, no, do not make yourself a meal! Do not make a meal of yourself!'

She grinned.

Then, as she looked down the temporarily deserted corridor, the grin faded and a look of resolution took its place. She's called Mrs Mullan, Megan told herself. She's a real, live, flesh-and-blood woman, and you're going to prove it to yourself before another day passes.

Susie was still on duty at reception. 'Megan – are you all right?'

'I am,' said Megan briskly, her tone disallowing further questions. 'But how about that Mrs Mullan – how did she hold up to having a grown woman, and a nurse at that, keel over at the very sight of her?'

Susie smiled uncertainly.

'Is she still here? I'd like to see her.'

'You don't have to worry about her. Charlie

should be finished stitching her up by now.'

'Where, love?'

'Cubicle two. Are you sure you're all right?'

'I'm fine. But I need to . . . lay a ghost, you might say.'

Megan didn't believe in ghosts, and her mother was more than thirty years dead. She knew that. But what she knew intellectually couldn't compete with something she had seen and felt – some deep part of her, primitive and pre-logical, was convinced that she had been visited by her mother. For what purpose she didn't like to think.

'There you are, Mrs Mullan. You'll be wielding a tin-opener again in no time,' said Charlie Fairhead cheerfully.

'Need any help?' asked Megan. It was something to say. She knew Charlie didn't need her help . She looked straight at the patient, Mrs Mullan, as she spoke.

A round-faced, Irish lass of about thirty; she'd be pretty if she looked happier. She looked vaguely familiar – but it was in type rather than detail. Her mother had been of this type, but this was not her mother.

'Are you all right?' asked Mrs Mullan.

Megan nodded. 'I came to tell you that . . . I didn't want you to think that it had anything to do with you – my fainting, I mean. It didn't have anything to do with you at all.'

'I thought it might have been the blood,' said Mrs Mullan. 'It nearly made *me* faint. But then I thought, if I faint, who'll know? I might bleed to death if I faint. My husband works nights, you see, and he wouldn't find me for hours. So I knew I couldn't faint. I had to look after myself because no one else would, otherwise.'

She wasn't even Irish. Her accent was pure Birmingham.

'That's right,' said Megan nodding. 'That's a good, sensible girl.'

'Not using a knife as a tin-opener in the first place would have been even more sensible,' said Charlie, low-voiced.

She doesn't look like my mother at all, Megan thought, and said aloud, 'Dear God, I *am* tired. Dreaming with my eyes open, that's what it was.'

'Go on home and go to bed,' said Charlie. 'I think I can cover you for the last ten minutes of the shift.'

'I'll bet you say that to all the girls! Goodnight, Charlie.'

'Good morning, Megan.'

Ted was waiting for her in his cab when she emerged from the hospital.

'You're early,' she said, getting in.

'So are you.'

'Quiet night.' She kissed his cheek and then lingered a moment, enjoying the closeness, his familiar warmth, the slight roughness of stubble on his face.

He was solid and real, and she was reluctant to break contact.

When, at last, she pulled back, Ted rubbed his cheek. 'Need a shave,' he said, voice apologetic.

Megan shrugged. 'Everybody needs something. Me, I need sleep.'

'And coffee.'

'And a nice, hot bath.'

'And bed.'

'Mmmm,' said Megan. 'And bed.'

# Chapter Two

The house was quiet when Ted and Megan returned home. Megan knew at once that their three sons must still be asleep.

'Ah, peace,' she said, stretching her arms luxuriously and sighing. 'I can remember a time when I wouldn't have believed it possible this house could be so calm and peaceful with our boys at home! Means our boys have grown up.'

Ted gave her a disbelieving look. 'Means our boys are sleeping is what it means,' he said. 'There's still no peace when they're awake.' He glanced at the sunburst clock above the cooker. 'I hope you've had enough of the quiet because it's about to end. Time our Dave was up, getting ready for work; I'll give him a shout.'

Dave was their eldest, nearly twenty-one. He'd been working as a driver for his father's cab company for the past six months, his shift beginning at about the time his father's ended.

Megan put the kettle on and began getting eggs, butter and bacon together for breakfast with the ease of long practice. She even hummed a tune to herself.

The night's events, hospital life, and even her own personal worries all faded away as she eased back into the ongoing, normal, infinitely comforting life of her family.

'He's not in his bed – it hasn't been slept in!' Ted announced, stomping back into the kitchen, glowering.

Megan didn't pause in her routine, deftly laying rashers of bacon on the grill. 'Well, you know where he spent the night, then.'

'At that girl's. It's getting to be a habit!'

Megan smiled. 'Is that so bad? Some habits are good ones – like us.'

'It's nothing like us. He's never going to marry her – why should he, when she lets him have what he wants?'

'Lets him have what he wants –' Megan turned around, hands on hips, and stared at the man she'd married twenty-three years before. 'Ted Roach, is that what you think marriage is about, after all this time? Did I ever put the price of marriage on my body before I'd let you touch me?'

Ted looked slightly abashed, but still he protested; 'I never spent the night with you before we were married!'

'You would if you could . . . and I'd have let you! It was only because of me living with my brother, and you living with your folks. If I'd been sharing a flat with another girl, the way Anabel is, there'd have been no one to mind if I stayed out all night. Anabel and Dave have been going out with each other for two years now. They're obviously serious about each other . . . just the way we were. Don't try to make out that we were such a pure-minded couple of young-sters . . . or that it was because I was so much better than Anabel that you married me.'

'Of course you were better than Anabel . . . you still are, and you always will be,' said Ted, his voice rough with the difficulty of expressing his feelings. 'That girl isn't good enough for our Dave, and he ought to know that, having a mother like you.'

Megan had a lump in her throat. She knew Ted loved her; although he seldom said as much in words, she didn't feel unappreciated. She had never been the type to need or demand verbal reassurance. And yet, sometimes, she had a longing to hear the words, even if they weren't absolutely necessary. Ted knew that, too, she thought. At that moment she loved him so much she couldn't speak.

The kettle began to whistle. Ted leaned past her and switched it off.

'Let's go to bed,' he said. 'Breakfast can wait.'

'But Tom and Bernard . . .'

'They won't be up for hours, lazy sods.' He put his arm around her and propelled her gently through the door. 'It's still quiet. That doesn't happen very often. Let's make the most of it.'

\*

14

Susie and Duffy had their heads together at reception when Megan walked in that evening. She knew by the guilty look on Duffy's face, and the way they moved apart, that they had been talking about her.

'Carry on gossiping, girls,' Megan said briskly. 'Don't let *me* stop you.'

'How are you, Megan?' Duffy asked.

'I'm fine. Consult the stars if you don't want to take my word for it – I'm a Virgo.'

'Virgo!' said Duffy, brightening. 'I knew it! I could have guessed! It's to do with your being so efficient, and so dedicated to doing your duty to other people.'

Megan gave her a disbelieving smile and began to move away.

'Oh, Megan,' Susie said, stopping her. 'Mr Plimmer said he wanted to see you when you came in.'

'I thought he was taking tonight off?'

Susie shrugged. 'He is, he says . . . he just dropped by, he said. Clearing up some paperwork. Won't be more than an hour.'

Megan looked at Duffy. 'Do you suppose he's a Virgo, too?'

Ewart Plimmer was standing, and had his coat on, when Megan entered his office.

'Oh, Megan, good,' he said. 'I hoped to see you before I left –'

'You shouldn't be here at all,' she said. 'You're not meant to be working tonight. You're taking Ros out to dinner . . . and to the cinema. *Amadeus*, I believe you said.'

'It's a late show. And there were just a few things I had to clear up first.'

'None of which could wait until tomorrow, I suppose?'

'It's very unfair of you to scold me, Megan, when I was intending to scold you.'

'They say the best defence is a good offence,' Megan said. They smiled at each other in a moment of mutual understanding.

'I was going to suggest you might want to have some time off,' Ewart said. 'Maybe you've been working too hard.'

'I may have to take some time off,' Megan said reluctantly. She sighed, knowing she would have to tell him, and steeling herself against his sympathy. 'It's not because I've been working too hard, though. It's – well, I went in for a routine exam and had a cervical smear taken. I've had the results. Positive. Not just an abnormality; it's a class four. Biopsy recommended.'

'Not just recommended,' said Ewart. 'Imperative. You must do it at once. No waiting; if you need any strings pulled, I'll –' he moved towards the phone as if he would deal with the matter immediately.

Megan shook her head at him. 'Do you think I couldn't pull strings on my own behalf? A cone biopsy . . . they could do it for me here, upstairs, some afternoon next week. I wouldn't feel like working that night, but I could take my day off . . .'

'Megan, don't be silly! Take off all the time you need!'

'One night,' she said. 'Maybe two . . . it's a biopsy, Ewart, not major surgery. I'm not going to stay in hospital overnight, taking up a bed somebody else needs.'

'Who has a better right than you?'

The concern in his voice threatened to shake her self-control. 'Ewart, please,' she said. 'Don't start . . . I don't want this to be a big production. I want to get through it with as little fuss as possible. No one else is to know.'

He frowned, but nodded. 'I won't say anything, of course. That's up to you. But Ted . . .'

'I haven't told Ted . . . yet. Don't give me that look, Ewart! Of course I'll tell him . . . when I have to. There's no sense in upsetting him unnecessarily. Look at us, we're professionals, and we can't even say the word. Cancer. That's what I have. Until AIDS came along, cancer was the worst anyone could imagine, the worst thing that could happen to you. A death sentence.'

'Don't be absurd! Whether it's your cervix or your uterus it can be treated. You know it's not . . .'

'I know it's not, and you know it's not, but we know what Ted's going to think as soon as he hears that word, no matter what I say afterwards, no matter

how I try to soften it. I tell him they found "carcinoma in situ" and he's going to say what's that
mean, and then I say cancer . . . The biopsy will tell us
how bad it is, and if it has spread or is likely to. If I'm
lucky, please God, the biopsy will be not only the
test but the cure as well. I won't be quite as good as
new, but I'll still be all there, with only a slightly
damaged cervix to show there was ever anything
wrong. I'd like to be able to go home and tell Ted
that I had a test done, and while they were doing it
they found some abnormal cells and removed
them . . . I want to be able to tell him truthfully that
there's nothing to worry about. If I must have a hysterectomy, I'll tell him then, but only once it's certain.'

'But why not tell him now? Let him know the pos-
sibilities. You could explain it to him, surely.'

'Why should I tell him when I don't have to? Why
make him worry? Maybe I have to have nightmares
– but he doesn't. Having him worry isn't going to
make it any easier for me – in fact, it will make it
harder, if I have to feel his fear as well as my own.'

'It's up to you, of course,' said Ewart. 'Just don't
take too much on your own shoulders. Sometimes it
helps to share. Sometimes it's better not to be alone.'

They looked at each other in silence. Outside the
room, Megan could hear footsteps in the corridor,
and low voices, then Clive King's unmistakable
laugh. The clock on the wall gave a buzzing click,
and Ewart looked up guiltily.

'Go on,' said Megan. 'Go share your free time with Ros.'

But an hour later, Ewart was still there. Megan bumped into him in the corridor as she was entering a cubicle. To her surprise, he followed her in.

'Megan, have you seen a youngish man in a tweed jacket and a trendy shirt – looks like a hairdresser wandering around on his own?'

Megan shook her head, preparing to wash her hands. 'Sounds like he needs help.'

If Ewart knew she had made a joke he gave no indication. 'If you see Kuba, tell him to see Susie straight away.'

'What's up?'

'Spot check.'

Megan smiled at the woman sitting on the trolley. 'That's hospital jargon for "something's wrong",' she said.

The patient, who was heavily pregnant, did not look impressed.

'You wait there, love, and someone will see to you soon.'

'Wait, wait, wait,' said the woman sourly. 'That's what they all say. What else *can* I do but wait?'

Megan heard Baz call her name as she stepped into the corridor, and found the doctor standing in administration with King.

'Megan. I want to keep Mrs Pearce in for twenty-four hours. Can you get her a bed in Obs?'

Megan gave her a look.

'I know, I know. But she's due in ten days and complaining of labour pains . . . better safe than sorry.'

Megan shrugged. Baz was over-reacting, but she couldn't tell her so. 'Charlie's in the ambulance bay. Young girl with head injury.'

'Thanks.'

When she had gone, Megan turned to King. 'Would you believe it? Young lady wants her baby induced 'cause it doesn't fit in with her holiday plans. She's tired of waiting, that's all. Baz wants to give her a bed; I'd give her a good talking-to and send her home. But Baz . . . put that woman in front of a pregnant mother and she loses her head.'

King walked away without a word.

Megan stared after him. 'Thanks for the chat,' she said. She headed for the phone.

'The ever-inspiring challenge of getting a bed,' she muttered to herself. 'The DHSS giveth, and it taketh away.'

Arguing with the ward sister about the availability of beds, Megan let none of her own reservations show, but battled just as fiercely for Mrs Pearce's right to a bed as if she were one of her own children. She was aware, with a small fraction of her attention, of a minor drama going on in the waiting room.

One young man shouted for help as another, dressed only in a towel, rolled on the floor, clutching at his side, obviously in agony.

Susie came running from the reception desk to help, just as Ewart – with the natty young man from the DHSS in tow – arrived. Ewart assessed the situation and took charge immediately.

'Deep breaths,' said Ewart, crouching on the floor beside the nearly-nude man. 'Nice and slow. That's it. That's it. Nice and slow. Stethoscope.'

Susie ran back to her desk and found a stethoscope, ran back and handed it to Ewart, just as Kuba, the model of efficiency, appeared on the scene with the trolley.

'Keep breathing in and out,' said Ewart. 'Slowly, slowly, nice and deep. In and out. In. Out. That's good, nice and deep. Right. Painful there?'

The young man nodded, wincing.

'What were you doing?'

'We were playing squash,' said his companion. 'We'd just finished a hard set when Jonathan's heart . . .'

'Ah. Pushed yourself a bit too hard?'

He nodded, his face crumpled in fear.

'You're going to be all right,' Ewart said firmly. 'Don't worry. Now . . . we've got to get you on to a trolley.' He looked at Kuba. 'Ready?' Working together, they lifted the young man on to the trolley.

'What did you go as?' Ewart asked, trying to disguise the effort it took to lift him. 'Lawrence of Arabia?' He indicated the young man's scanty costume.

'Huh? Oh, no, I fell down in the showers . . . Richard, my mate there, I think he's got my clothes. I didn't want to waste time getting dressed. I was too scared; I thought . . .'

'No need to be scared now,' said Ewart. 'You're in good hands.'

'Right, off we go,' said Kuba, and began steering the trolley down the corridor towards the crash room.

Megan hung up the phone. A temporary stalemate about the bed; she'd return to do battle later. For the moment, she was needed in the crash room. Mrs Pearce would just have to settle in for more waiting.

Baz, Charlie and Duffy were in one half of the crash room, attending to a little girl who had been brought in with a head injury. As Megan entered, Charlie nodded towards the scantily-clad young man.

'He needs hooking up, plus the usual.'

Ewart stepped aside with Baz as the nurses worked. 'Seems fine. Fast, of course, but he's scared.'

'History?'

'Jonathan Potter. Fell down in the shower . . . hence the strange garb. Friend Richard helped get him here, and then he collapsed in the waiting room.'

Baz nodded, taking it in. 'Right.'

Ewart looked from the little girl to Jonathan, and then back at Baz, apologetic. 'I'd stay, but . . .'

'Bob Baker of the DHSS needs your attention, far

more urgently, I know.'

Still Ewart hesitated. 'How's the girl?'

'Stable enough.'

'Can you cope?'

'If I can't, I'll call the Night Registrar. Which I believe is the correct procedure in such events . . . Mr Plimmer?'

Ewart smiled. 'May I quote you on that?'

'Tell Mr Baker he can rely on me.' She turned back to supervise the rest of the team, all working with the quiet efficiency which had developed from long practice as well as familiarity with each other.

Megan looked down at Jonathan, aware of his fear, working at soothing it away with her matter-of-fact manner and the warmth in her voice. She showed him the E.C.G. pads before attaching them. 'These may feel a bit cold . . . lucky you being in the shower, wasn't it? Lucky for us, I mean. You wouldn't believe the number of clothes some people come in wearing – just as you think you're finally getting down to skin, you find another layer. Now, I've got to get some of your blood for samples. That isn't going to bother you, is it? No, I didn't think so. You're a brave lad, aren't you? And young and strong. I know it must have been frightening for you, but you needn't worry now you're here. We do the worrying now. Just you relax and we'll take care of the details . . .'

She glanced at the heart monitor as she spoke. Jonathan had calmed – he wasn't quite so frightened any longer. Now the heart monitor showed that both the rhythm and rate of his heart were perfectly normal.

She transferred the blood into three separate bottles for toxicology, and labelled them as Baz told her what was needed.

'Blood sugar. Haemaglobin. And a mineral count.'

'A.S.A.P?'

'Yup.'

Megan paused long enough to give Jonathan a smile. 'Cheer up, love, it's looking better all the time,' she said, and then took the samples off to be analysed .

Charlie had also been watching the heart monitor, and now he drew Baz aside. 'What are you going to say?'

'What can I say? I can wait for the blood count to come back, but it's clear already that he's perfectly normal.'

'Except that he's terrified out of his wits.'

'Just what I need,' said Baz, in obvious irritation. 'A healthy patient convinced he's dying.'

'The pain was real enough when he felt it.'

'Muscle cramp,' said Baz with a shrug. 'Or I'm wrong.'

'What do we say about the twitching?'

'That'll pass.'

'You sure?'

'If it doesn't, tell him to come back.' She moved

away from Charlie, to Jonathan, who looked nervous at her approach. 'How do you feel?'

'Pain's gone.'

'Good.'

'How's my heart?'

'Fast, but otherwise perfectly sound.'

'What?'

'It wasn't a heart attack,' Baz said. 'Probably just a muscle spasm. You said you were playing squash . . .'

Jonathan looked alarmed. 'I wasn't pretending, I wasn't putting it on back there, you know.'

'No, I'm sure it must have hurt.'

'It was serious. *You* took it seriously.'

'We always do.'

'Oh, no, you mean I'm all right?'

Baz bit her lip and looked down at his file. 'Fit as a fiddle.'

'But I can't be! You must be hiding something . . . tell me the truth!'

'Mr Potter, I wouldn't lie to you. We're doing some blood tests, which will be ready in about ten minutes. All being well – and we have no reason to expect that it won't be – you can then go home.'

'I can't! I've got to be ill!'

Baz stared at him in disbelief. Most people refused to believe there was anything wrong with them. Even the most raging hypochondriacs displayed relief when told that their suspected heart attacks or stomach cancers were nothing to worry about. They might always believe they were ill, but they didn't want to be. 'Why?'

'I'll look such an idiot,' he said, in a low voice full of misery.

'Not at all. You were quite right to be worried, and to come in.'

'You tell him that.'

'Who?'

'Richard. He'll never let me live it down.'

'Nice friends you have,' said Charlie.

'He drinks more, eats more, talks more, makes love more . . . it'll make his day.'

Charlie looked at Baz, who shrugged. He had a sudden inspiration. 'Not if you have these.' He plucked a small sample bottle off a shelf and stuck a label on it. Taking his pen from his jacket pocket, he wrote something on it. 'Anti-pectoritus tablets. Take two daily. Two of these daily and you live, forget one – you die, slowly.'

Jonathan looked hopeful. Baz held up a cautioning hand.

'But,' she said, 'only if you promise not to do the brave bit again. You don't have to outdo your friends in everything, especially not in heart attacks. Next time it just might be more serious. Your body is trying to tell you something when it hurts. And if you hurt, you should tell someone, OK?'

Jonathan nodded, and looked again at Charlie. 'What was that name you used?'

'Pectoritus. Tell your friend it's a famous German condition.'

'And what are the tablets?'

Charlie shook the bottle, which made no sound. 'It's empty. You supply the Smarties. Now, shall we unplug?'

Megan met Baz back in the administration area, and gave her the results of Jonathan's blood tests. Baz hardly looked at them; that crisis was over, and another had taken its place. She was inspecting X-rays of the little girl's ribs, holding them up to the light.

'Long bone fracture,' she said to Megan. 'That'll need an operation, but no parents, no consent, no operation.'

'Kuba's with the other girl,' Megan said. 'Maybe she'll tell him something, tell him who to phone.'

'Kuba will make her a cup of hot chocolate and tell her about Poland, and she'll just sit there without a word,' Baz said. 'King's the one who's good with kids – King should be talking to her now. Have you seen him?'

Megan shook her head. 'I'll go look for him.'

'He should be on duty,' said Baz. She looked back at the X-rays, frowning.

The staffroom was dark, but it wasn't empty. Megan switched on the light and stared at King. 'What were you doing with the light off?'

'Eh, I had a bit of a migraine,' he said. He looked

27

uncomfortable, not meeting her gaze.

Megan closed the door behind her and went to put the kettle on. 'Taken a tablet?' she asked.

'Don't like tablets.'

Filling the kettle, she said, 'Kuba's in the porter's lodge with a kid who won't talk. We need a name and address. Sounds like a case for Clive King.'

He stood up to go.

'It can wait another minute. Sit down.'

She turned back and watched him sit. His face was closed and sullen. 'What's going on?'

'Nothing I can't handle on my own,' he said.

'It doesn't look like that from where I'm standing.'

His eyes flashed to meet hers angrily. 'What are you implying?'

Megan cocked her head and said in an accent that was heavily Irish, 'Do you mind if I do the Wise Old Woman Act for a minute?'

King smiled, and Megan all but applauded. 'My God, he smiled. Progress at last. The way you've been treating me like an enemy lately, I was beginning to wonder. Although yesterday, when I fainted – yes, you remember that? Do you remember what you told me, about looking after myself? You were, right, although I hate to admit it. And I am going to look after myself – I'm not going to run away from my problem, or pretend it isn't happening to me. I'm going to take care of myself as if I were any other patient. I don't think it's too much to ask the same thing of you.'

'What are you talking about?'

'King. You're drinking and I know it. Now don't stiffen like that! The world has not yet come to an end, and I am not about to run to Ewart's office shouting, "King's a drinker". A, because I know at heart you're really not, and B, because Ewart wouldn't have any choice if I did. You'd be out. Full stop. End of story. Now, as I see it, you've got a simple choice. You stop now, before it gets ridiculous . . . take some leave, sort it out, whatever you need to do. Or, you continue as you have been. And sometime, maybe not this week, maybe not even this month, but sometime, you are going to cock it up. And you are experienced enough to know what that means.'

King said nothing. Megan watched him, waiting. The kettle came to a boil and switched itself off. Still nothing from King.

'Talk to me,' she said, very gently.

'There's nothing to say.'

'Come on, King! Don't do that to me! How long have we known each other? Fifteen years? Tell me what's going on.'

'Am I a good nurse?'

Megan nodded, rather surprised that he needed to ask. 'Everyone on this team is good. Oddball, perhaps, but good.'

'How do you rate Charlie?'

Megan frowned, sensing something behind the

question but not quite sure of its shape. But whatever his reason for asking, he must know she would give an honest answer. 'He's one of the best. Why?'

King shrugged and stood up. 'I'm on duty, I've got to go.'

'Wait. Talk to me, King, please. Is this something to do with Charlie?'

'Megan, I appreciate what you're trying to do. But leave it. Please.' He paused, then met her eye and said, 'It's under control. I just need some space.'

Megan nodded slowly. 'If space is what you need, I'll try to give it to you. But it would be better for you – for all of us – if it's me you were explaining yourself to, and not Ewart Plimmer. Remember, next time this might not be private.'

Her words made no impact. He had shut himself up again. 'Where did you say the kid was?'

'Porter's Lodge.' She watched him go. She had done all she could. Nursing was based on the idea of helping people. But Megan had learned, as the mother of three sons, that you couldn't always help others – there were times when all you could do was step back, and let them help themselves, or – and this was much harder – let them go to hell in their own way. People had to make their own choices and live their own lives. You could let them know you were on their side, but you couldn't do the work for them. It was up to Clive to rescue himself – if he would.

# Chapter Three

The night was far from over. Megan had just prepared herself a much-wanted cup of tea when Duffy burst into the staffroom.

'Crash room,' she said.

Megan put the cup down, untasted. 'The little girl?'

Duffy nodded as they went out together. 'Started speeding during the X-rays.'

They began to run, and reached the crash room at the same time as Baz and Charlie.

'Abdomen's tight,' said Baz. Charlie looked up from checking the girl's pulse.

'Ruptured spleen?'

Megan saw Baz's affirmative nod and asked, 'Peritoneal lavage or cannula?'

'Give me a cannula,' said Baz. 'Blood pressure, Duffy. Charlie, ring for theatre. We need parental consent immediately.'

'King's with the other girl now,' said Megan.

'Tell him he's got about five minutes, or we go ahead without.'

Megan made sure that Baz had the equipment she

needed, and that Duffy was close by to help her before she moved away. 'Ring Ewart?' she asked, as a second thought.

Baz didn't look up from her work. 'Leave him for the moment.'

'Blood pressure, one hundred over forty,' said Duffy.

'Damn! Why didn't I see it before?' Baz exclaimed, as Megan walked swiftly away with her message to King.

Inside the Porter's Lodge, Kuba's video was showing a cartoon, but no one was watching it. Kuba was hovering, looking lost and concerned, out of his element as he so often was. Megan wondered briefly if there was any situation, anywhere in the world where Kuba *would* seem at home. His face brightened at the sight of her, but he said nothing. King was crouched on the floor beside the little girl who huddled in the moulded plastic chair, clutching a Darth Vadar helmet as if it were a teddy-bear.

'Listen to me,' said King. 'They'll be so worried about you they'll be glad to hear from you – they'll just be happy you're alive.'

The girl did not respond. King stood up as Megan came in, eyes questioning her.

'She's ruptured her spleen,' Megan murmured.

'How long have I got?'

'Five minutes.'

'Leave her with me.'

Megan nodded. 'Kuba,' she said, inclining her head. Kuba followed her out.

'You think Clive can get her to talk?'

'He knows kids,' said Megan. 'If he can't, nobody can. Now, Kuba, just leave him to it. I've got to get back and tend to her sister.'

Within seconds, King had performed his usual miracle with the silent child – Megan never did learn how he managed it – and had a name and phone number. Parental consent was obtained, and Megan was able to see the patient into the operating theatre, knowing that everything possible would be done for her. She was in good hands.

The next case was far less satisfying, one of the minor tragedies of which hospital life was full. A seriously disturbed woman came in with a baby asking for medicine, but reluctant to let anyone else touch the child. It turned out that the baby, was not her own, and when Baz finally managed to get the infant away from the woman, it was too late. The baby had been dead for at least an hour – long before the woman brought her in to hospital. All the skills of a highly-trained staff were useless in the face of this simple fact, and it cast a temporary pall over them all, a sense of the vast unfairness of life, and of their own human weakness before death.

Megan felt it strongly – she was, after all, a mother herself – but she didn't brood about it. Although this might be seen by others as a good, professional attitude to have, it went deeper than that for Megan. She'd had an early acquaintance with death, when first a younger brother, and then her mother, had died. It had not soured her own life. Instead, it had reinforced her feeling for the importance of life, and the necessity of carrying on rather than giving in. Her mother had died – but her father and two brothers lived on, and their lives, like her own, were important. The dead were beyond her reach; but she knew that she could help the living, and so she must.

She walked away from the dead baby, out of the crash room, and said to Charlie, when she met him, 'Never stood a chance.'

Then she said to Susie, in the same matter-of-fact tone, 'Who's next?'

Mr Thompson was next, limping on what Megan suspected was simply a badly bruised foot. She was cheerful, calm and comforting and sent him off to X-ray just to be sure that nothing had been broken when he fell off his bike.

It was nearly three o'clock in the morning before Megan managed to get to the staffroom for her long-delayed cup of tea, and to eat a sandwich. It was a quiet time, so most of the rest of the staff took advantage of it and had a break then, too. She met King on the way, and they entered together. Duffy and Baz were already there, and Charlie was playing tea-lady.

'Is one of those for me?' asked Megan, eyeing the steaming mugs.

'Help yourself.'

She did, and looked around for the sugar bowl. It was empty except for a few stray grains at the bottom. She gave Charlie a challenging look. 'Whose turn was it to buy the sugar?'

'Guilty,' said Charlie, letting his shoulders and eyebrows sag mournfully.

'I might have guessed.' She sighed regretfully, then looked resigned. 'Oh, well, I guess it's good for me, cutting down on sweets.'

'I've a bar of chocolate you can have,' Charlie said.

'To melt in my tea? No thanks.' She settled into a chair and unwrapped her sandwich just as Ewart Plimmer entered with Kuba.

There were no chairs left, so they both remained standing beside the door.

Megan looked at her watch, and then at Ewart. 'So, did Ros have to go to the cinema by herself, then?'

'I did phone her,' he said. From his voice Megan guessed that Ros had not taken the news of yet another cancelled engagement at all well. Although the woman ought to be used to it by now, she thought. After so many years of being married to a man as dedicated – or obsessed – as Ewart, Ros surely couldn't expect him to start slowing down now just because her own career was now making fewer demands on her time. Still, no one could go on being 'understanding' forever . . . eventually there came the straw that broke the camel's back.

Ewart looked around the crowded room. 'If I could just have a word . . . I won't keep you long, but I thought I ought to fill you in on the spot check. I think tonight has proved, if proof was ever necessary, just what kind of mentality we're up against in our fight to save this department. In short, they don't like us.

'I think it would be counterproductive and a waste of breath to start dishing out blame for the cock-up with Baker tonight. Clearly he should not have been allowed to wander around alone. That was my fault, but next time I might not be here. All I'm asking you to do is stay sharp and keep each other informed.

'Oh, and if you could see your way to stealing a little less from Lawson's ward – naming no names Megan.'

Megan choked on her tea. She kept her eyes down.

'I think that'd be appreciated by the powers that be,' Ewart continued. 'Obviously, in the heat of the moment, you may find yourself forgetting what I've just said . . . but in that case, try to spread the net a bit. The fact that Lawson's ward is the closest – just down the corridor – hasn't been missed.'

Ewart looked around. Both King and Charlie were grinning.

'Seriously,' said Ewart. 'We've got to watch our step. I know the patients come first, but the bureaucrats are watching us, and they've a day shift staff whose jobs on this department may depend on how well we perform. Basically, all I'm saying is, be as good as you can. I believe the song is entitled, "We Shall Overcome".'

Kuba burst into applause. Gradually, looking either sheepish or ironic, the others all set aside their mugs of tea to join in.

Susie appeared behind Ewart, and looked in at Baz. 'The mother's here,' she said.

Baz tensed, and Megan realized that Susie must be talking about the mother of the dead baby. Megan wasn't the only one to realize that Baz couldn't cope with telling the mother that her baby hadn't survived her ordeal. She saw Charlie register this as well, and get to his feet, saying to Susie, 'I'll talk to her.'

Good lad, Charlie, she thought.

Susie nodded. 'She's waiting out front, with the police.' She touched Ewart's shoulder. 'Your wife's just arrived – she's gone through to your office.'

'Thank you, Susie,' said Ewart. He didn't look happy as he left. Megan had a strong intuition that tonight had been the straw that broke Ros's back.

'Poor Ewart,' said Susie, confirming Megan's suspicion. 'She was carrying a suitcase and a carrier bag full of his clothes. I don't know how he'll cope without her.'

'If Ewart could convince the DHSS that this team of ours was a good bet, he can surely convince his wife to give him another chance,' said Megan, finishing her cup of tea.

'Sounds like you're expecting miracles,' said King.

Megan heard the very personal bitterness in his tone. She looked at him steadily. 'I think we have to expect miracles,' she said. 'I think we can make miracles happen. Life itself is a miracle, sometimes.'

'Especially around here,' said Duffy.

# Chapter Four

It had been the wettest summer Holby had seen in twenty years, according to the radio announcers and other such authorities, but for one week at the end of September there came a sudden glorious burst of sunshine and high temperatures. With the sort of luck that doesn't usually happen, Megan had both the Saturday and the Sunday nights off that week.

'We ought to take advantage of this weather,' she said to her husband. 'I, for one, don't intend to sleep through it! I'd like to get away from the city, go somewhere the air's worth breathing, have a picnic, look at some scenery. Flowers would be nice . . . what do you say, love?'

The thought of nature never brought a smile to Ted's dour face. He was a city boy, born and bred, and their own back garden, and a generous helping of some well-cooked vegetable, was all he needed or wanted of green. His wife liked to see things growing, though. He knew that, even if he didn't understand it. It was one of those odd feminine fancies, he imagined, and because she so seldom asked for anything for herself he was pleased when she gave him the opportunity to indulge her.

Not that he would show his pleasure, of course.

'Well,' he said, as if giving the matter careful thought, 'I had been meaning to lag the pipes. With winter coming on, it needs to be done, and we wouldn't want to leave it too late. Still, I expect we could go somewhere on Sunday. With this weather. Somewhere nice, outdoors. Now where would that be?'

'I was thinking of Dyrham Park. Do you remember, we went there once with the Kilworths, when the boys were small. The house was nice, I remember – there were some tapestries, and a lot of blue and white Dutch pottery. And the gardens . . .' her face was wistful. 'That was a lovely day.'

'That must have been ten years ago, at least,' Ted said. 'Maybe more like twelve.'

She gave him a wry look. 'I don't think they've closed it down in the meantime. National Trust, I think.'

'All right, we'll go there,' he said. 'It's not too far, as I recall. It couldn't have been, if we dared to take the three sprogs.'

'Let's take them again,' Megan said impulsively. 'It would be lovely to go as a family . . . a proper outing.'

'They've probably already made plans,' Ted said. 'Tom and Bernard off with their mates, and Dave with that girl.'

'Don't say "that girl" – she has a name. And it

won't hurt to ask,' said Megan. 'They just might fancy a picnic with their old parents.'

As it happened, the boys did fancy a picnic, all three of them for once in agreement not only with each other, but with Megan and Ted. Dave asked if he could bring Anabel.

'Of course you can, love. Although it may be a bit of a squeeze,' she added, thinking of the car.

'No worries, I'll take my banger. That way, Tom and Bernie can pile in with us, and you and Dad can have a little peace, at least on the drive.'

'A rare commodity around here, peace,' said Megan. He was no longer a thoughtless boy, she thought, regarding her eldest son. He had grown into a man sensitive to the needs of others. She said, half-teasing, 'But how will the four of you ever agree on what music to have in the car? I thought you had such different tastes.'

'Oh, we do,' Dave agreed. 'That is, I've got taste – the others don't. But we've all got our private stereo systems.' He mimed the putting on of headphones. 'The greatest invention of the modern age!'

'I'm not so sure about that; it may stop you arguing, but it's murdered the art of conversation.'

'In our Tom's case, I'd say it was euthanasia, and we should be grateful.'

Megan chuckled appreciatively. 'Where do you learn all those big words?'

*

Dyrham Park was a late seventeenth-century house set in 263 acres of ancient parkland, some seven miles north of Bath, and very near the M4, which meant that the drive out took almost no time at all. The gardens were very beautiful, although not with the fecund, summertime splendour which Megan remembered from her previous visit, but rather with the mellow, slightly melancholy tints of autumn.

But it was appropriate, Megan thought, for she had changed, too, since her last visit. Then, she had been a young mother, past the springtime of her first youth, through with bearing children but devoted to nurturing and raising them. Now her family of sons did not need her in quite the same way. Her years both of bearing and of nurturing had passed; she was in the autumn of her life. But still autumn, she told herself firmly. Not yet winter. 'The season of mists and mellow fruitfulness,' she said aloud.

'What's that?' asked Ted.

'Autumn,' she said, smiling.

He still looked puzzled, but when she squeezed his hand he smiled back.

It was nice to wander through the high-ceilinged, solidly crafted, rather sparsely furnished rooms of Dyrham Park, to gaze at the old-fashioned paintings, the pretty blue and white Delftware and the dusty old tapestries, and imagine days gone by while Bernard read aloud from a guidebook, explaining the history of the rooms and objects which had long

42

ago belonged to William Blathwayt, Secretary of State to King William III.

Megan enjoyed herself – the peace and expensive, dignified beauty of the great house was so very different from what she was used to – but it was when they went outside, onto the great lawns and through the formal gardens, that she was happiest.

It was a nearly perfect day. The glorious weather, the beautiful surroundings, the nearness of those she loved best, all of them in harmony, all joined to produce one of those rare, memorable occasions which Megan knew she would always remember.

Ted and Tom spread out a cloth (although the grass felt surprisingly dry after so many weeks of rain) beneath a spreading shade tree, with a good view of the house, and Megan began to unpack her bags and baskets of provisions.

'You've made so much,' said Anabel, helping with the unpacking. 'We'll surely never manage to eat it all!' Dave's girlfriend was a university student, a thin, slight girl with a mop of dark red curls, and beautiful, heavily-made-up grey eyes. She seemed very sweet, Megan thought, and it was obvious that she thought the world of Dave, which predisposed Megan in her favour. It was her voice which had set Ted against her – she had a rather affected manner of speaking and a posh accent.

Megan smiled at her. 'Have you never seen these lads eat? A plague of locusts is nothing beside them!'

'Our Dave must have been on his best behaviour,' Ted said. Then, nodding at Anabel, 'Just you wait!' For their feast, Megan had made piles of sandwiches – chicken, ham, cheese and pickle, egg and tomato – as well as a sweetcorn, tuna and pasta salad, with hardboiled eggs, tomatoes and pickled onions. She'd also brought half a dozen bags of potato crisps and a bag full of apples and oranges. To drink, there were bottles of light ale and fizzy lemonade. It did look a lot of food, spread out on the cloth, but, true to Megan's prediction, all of it was consumed.

Feeling full and happy, Megan leaned back against the tree, and looked around at her family.

There was young Tom, dressed all in ragged black, a bright orange streak in his spiky hair speaking of his rebellion against society. Megan suspected he wanted to look fierce, but with his soft, innocent young face, whatever costume he wore was obviously simply a game of 'let's pretend'. She could gaze at him to her heart's content, for although physically present, her youngest son was miles away inside his head. He wore the ubiquitous small headphones, the tape player hooked to his belt, and his eyes were closed as he nodded his head along to the unheard music.

Bernard, her middle son, was also a million miles – or more – away. He was lying sprawled on his stomach amid the wreckage of the meal, and was reading one of the science fiction novels he loved so much. She didn't understand it. He had never done well at school, but two years ago the comics which had for so long been his preferred, almost only, reading matter had been displaced by books about alien monsters, space wars, and future societies. More recently, he had bought himself a second-hand typewriter, and started to write his own science fiction stories. Megan didn't believe it would ever come to anything. He would lose interest in science fiction as soon as he found a girlfriend. But for the time being it kept him busy and made life on the dole easier for him.

Dave and Anabel had moved away from the others. They were holding hands and walking slowly across the grass in the sunlight. Megan gazed after the young couple, aware of conflicting emotions. Dave was in love and it made him happy, and she had to be pleased by that. And yet although she tried to like Anabel for his sake, and would even defend the girl against Ted's grumblings, she couldn't help feeling, at the same time, a pang of hurt and jealousy. Her first-born had grown up and no longer needed her. He no longer loved her best of all. She had been displaced in his affections by a girl his own age.

It was natural and right. Megan knew that. But it still hurt. She supposed the hurt, too, was natural, and she knew she would get over it.

Children grew up. You couldn't keep them with

you forever. That was all part of life.

She looked at Ted, lying on his back, eyes closed, dozing, and felt grateful for his existence, for his continuing presence in her life. They had been through a lot together, she reflected, and they would go through much more. At that moment she decided to tell him about the results of her smear test, tell him that a biopsy would have to be done, share with him all the facts and her own fears about them. He would stand beside her as he had for years, as he had promised to do forever. He would make it easier to bear, whatever happened. She was being foolish, trying to bear it all on her own, she thought. She would tell him as soon as they were alone together.

It seemed easy when she made the decision. It seemed easy when it was still in the future. But after they had packed up their things, when she and Ted were alone together in the car, heading back to Holby, she didn't know how to begin. She didn't know what to say.

If only Ted would make some comment about her health, or say something she could respond to, something that might lead gently into the subject. But Ted said nothing. He was never one for small-talk. It always had been Megan who directed the conversation; why should today be any different?

She might wait forever if she was waiting for him, or for an easy way in. If she was going to tell him, she would just have to tell him. Megan gazed out the window at all the other cars, all the other people heading home after a day's outing. In each car some private drama was being played out, if only inside someone's head.

'I went to see the GP, you know, for the annual check-up,' she said, conversationally.

'Dr Evans?'

'He has a partner now, a young one. Dr Brooker. It was her I saw.'

'That's good. He's getting pretty old, Evans. I should think he'd be wanting to retire soon. All he did was talk about his grandchildren when I went in for my back that time. A partner. Hmm. A young woman? What'd you make of her?'

'Pretty girl. Very sure of herself . . . with cause, I think. A bit like Baz, but not so nervy. More relaxed. Of course, maybe Baz would be like that with regular surgery hours, instead of working in casualty.'

Ted made a faint sound of disbelief. Megan knew he didn't approve of Baz – as least, he spoke as if he didn't. She suspected that the truth was that he was intimidated by the beautiful and high-powered young woman.

But she was getting away from her subject; she had never meant to talk about Baz.

'Anyway, this Dr Brooker, she did some tests –'

'Tests?'

She thought she detected the hint of alarm in his voice, and said hastily, 'It's the usual thing for a woman of my age. Just routine. I've had them before. Only this time the results were different. Positive. Now, it might not be anything to worry about; in fact, I'm certain it's nothing to worry about. But they have to be sure . . . they want to do more tests.'

'Dr Brooker does?'

'Well, no, not Dr Brooker herself –'

'Maybe you should stick with Evans,' Ted said. 'We know him. He knows you. These young doctors . . . maybe they're too quick. Maybe they don't always know their business as well as someone who's been practising for more than thirty years.'

'It's not Dr Brooker, love,' Megan said gently. 'All she did was take the smear. It's the results. When the results are positive . . . then you need to do something about it.'

He stared straight ahead at the road, concentrating hard. 'And what do they need to do?'

'I told you, it's another test . . . but it's also the cure. It's called a biopsy. They need to take a piece of . . . of tissue, from inside me, so they can analyse the cells. And if they find the . . . the abnormality, they'll take it out right then. It's not very complicated; it won't take long. They'll do it for me one morning at City Hospital, and I'll be home in the afternoon. It's nothing for you to worry about.' Her voice was as warm and comforting as she knew how to make it.

Ted was still frowning through the windscreen,

not looking at her, but she could sense his concern.

'I don't understand these medical things,' he said apologetically.

'Well, there's no reason why you should!'

'And . . . and . . . it's not serious, this?'

'No, of course not,' Megan said firmly.

'Only, I can't help worrying . . .'

'Now, you're *not* to worry. I didn't tell you this to worry you! I'm not ill; I don't feel the least bit ill. It's only that one of my . . . my feminine bits and pieces . . . may have something wrong with it. And so it's only sensible to find out if it does, and have it taken care of.'

'You'll tell me if there's anything . . . anything I can do?'

'Anything you can do? You haven't been studying medicine, have you? Leave that to the doctors. And don't worry.'

Her tone was bracing and dismissive. Ted said nothing; there was really nothing for him to say. They were both silent as they drove into Holby through the cool twilight, towards the setting sun.

# Chapter Five

To everyone else, Megan appeared unflappable and unconcerned. She was in control, and there was nothing to worry about. As far as Ted and the boys and a few close friends knew, she was going in for some tests not because there was anything to worry about, but only as a sensible precaution. She was a nurse, after all, and knew about prevention. The word 'cancer' was never spoken, and perhaps no one but Megan even thought it. She gave the impression that the problem, if there was one, was simply a minor nuisance connected with the change of life. Certainly she looked healthy; rosy-cheeked, bright-eyed, as sturdy, efficient and cheerful as ever. Who would think to doubt her when Megan said that she was fine?

Ted might have his doubts, but he didn't know how to express them . . . and Megan wouldn't let him. Dave, Tom and Bernard accepted what Megan said at face value. They had never known their mother to be ill, beyond the occasional bout of 'flu, and the idea that they should worry about her simply never entered their minds. Mum looked after

Ted, Dave, Bernard, Tom, the two dogs, Ted's ailing mother, poor Mr Collee next door (since his wife had left) and any friend or stranger who had need of her services, either in hospital or out. Night or day she was always there with a comforting word, homely advice or practical aid. How could someone like that possibly be in need of help herself?

Dave's girlfriend Anabel was the only one to respond to the news of Megan's impending biopsy with obvious alarm.

Dave told her over a meal of fish and chips in the kitchen of her flat, the sound of 'Top of the Pops' coming to them from the next room where her flat-mates were having their own, rather noisier take-away meal.

Anabel's eyes widened.

'Don't look like that,' Dave protested. 'It's nothing to worry about; it's only a test.'

'A test, yes certainly; but don't you realize what it's a test *for*?'

Dave shrugged, speared a chip and dunked it in tomato sauce. 'Something to do with change of life, I think . . . I dunno about women's problems.'

'Well *I* do,' said Anabel. 'And a biopsy's nothing to do with your age. It's a test for cancer.'

'It can't – she doesn't –,' he swallowed. 'Well, any-way, it is just a test – just to make sure nothing's wrong. And I'm sure nothing's wrong. She's perfectly fine; she said so herself. Well, you saw her on Sunday.'

'If she's so healthy, what does she need a biopsy for?'

'Well, I dunno, do I? Better safe than sorry, I suppose. Doctors are always giving people tests. Probably to do with her change of life – that's what she said – because she's not so young as she once was.'

Anabel shook her head. 'A biopsy's not like a blood test – they don't just give them to everyone. If a doctor has ordered a biopsy it must be because her cervical smear was positive . . .'

'Positive,' Dave said, nodding. 'That's what she said – something about her pap test being positive. But that's not bad, is it?'

'If the pap test – that's the cervical smear – is negative, that's good, it means there's nothing wrong. If it's positive it means there's some question, some abnormality. It might be nothing . . . they'll try again. That happened to me once – I was really scared, but it turned out I'd had an infection which interfered with the results.'

'So it could be nothing . . .'

'They don't order a biopsy for nothing. They must have found something definite, more than just an abnormality; a definite carcinoma.'

Dave glared at her. They had both stopped eating. From the sitting room came the high, clear voice of Annie Lennox singing about 'The Miracle of Love'.

'What do you know about it?' he demanded. 'You may be at university, but that doesn't mean you know everything. French is your speciality, not medicine. My mother happens to be a nurse – she's the expert, not you. If there's a chance she might have cancer, she'd know it.'

'I'm sure she does know.'

'Then why-'

'She probably doesn't want you worrying. After all, there's nothing you can do. And the biopsy might clear it up. If it's only local, if it hasn't spread past the cervix, they can treat it right then. If they've caught it early enough, it may be all right.'

'Thanks a lot.' He pushed his meal aside.

'David.' She caught his arm, but he wouldn't look at her. 'David, I *care*. About you, and about Megan. I'm not trying to frighten you –'

'Oh no?'

'I just think you ought to know what's really happening. It doesn't do you, or her, any good to hide your head in the sand.'

'Why didn't she tell me, then?'

'Maybe she thought you didn't want to know. Maybe because you're still her little boy, and she wasn't sure how you'd cope with it . . .'

Dave shook his head hard, rejecting it all. 'She would have told me,' he said. 'She didn't, so you're wrong. It's not true,' he said. 'There's nothing wrong with my mother. There can't be.'

Anabel watched him, love and sadness in her eyes.

The sound of pop music from the next room suddenly cut off, and Gwyneth stuck her fuzzy yellow head around the door. 'We're off down the pub – coming?'

'Sure,' said Dave, standing up, 'Why not?' He dumped his fish and chips into the rubbish bin. 'Come on, Anabel. Eat, drink and be merry, for tomorrow we may die.'

Megan presented a bold face to the world, and almost believed her own propaganda. Sure, everything would be fine. A cone biopsy wasn't exactly a day at the seaside, but it wasn't anything to fret about either. Not when you considered the alternatives.

She was lucky she'd had the test which discovered the carcinoma; lucky to be of an age that a cervical smear was thought necessary. If she'd been ten years younger, she might even now be dying in ignorance. Although cervical cancer was becoming more and more common in younger women, and Megan knew that many experts recommended that women should have their first smear taken when they became sexually active and after that at least once every three years, the National Health Service policy had it otherwise. GPs were only paid to perform cervical smears once every five years, and only on women considered most at risk – women who were over thirty-five, or had had at least three pregnancies.

Duffy and some of the other nurses at City Hospital had taken part in a campaign agitating for change in NHS policy, regarding regular cervical smears for all women, and Megan had allowed herself to be lectured to, listening sympathetically, but not feeling especially involved. There were so many areas in which people needed an expansion of health services, but nothing seemed to make an impact on a government which seemed more concerned with saving money than with saving lives.

'No one has to die of cervical cancer,' Duffy had said. 'But women do. It can be treated when it's caught in time – and the earlier it's caught, the simpler the treatment. And the simpler the treatment, the less time spent in hospital, the cheaper it is . . . in the long run, regular cervical smears for all woman won't just save lives, its would also save money.'

It's saved me, Megan told herself on the morning that she went in for her biopsy. NHS policy has its flaws, but I can be grateful because this time it worked for me.

Lying on the trolley, waiting to be given the anaesthetic, Megan's mind drifted to an image she often called on in times of stress, when she wanted to calm herself.

A little, low, old white cottage nestled in the luxuriant green Irish countryside. It was the sight that still spelled home to Megan, although she had not actually seen it in nearly a quarter of a century.

No one she knew now lived there, if the house itself even still stood. But it was there in her mind, this most potent image from her past. There, with the garden in front of it, so real she could almost smell the honeysuckle growing up the wall beside the door. There were lupins and tulips, violets and sweet-peas too. Flowers everywhere, all colours, the living sign of her mother's green fingers. And there was her mother, standing in the doorway, smiling at her. Megan smiled back.

'Looks like you're half asleep already,' said the anaesthetist. 'You're a calm customer . . . don't get many in here who start out smiling . . . here, now, pleasant dreams . . .'

Megan heard the voice of the anaesthetist, and was aware of him standing at her side. And then she felt another presence – was it the consultant?

Fighting against the gathering mists of unconsciousness, Megan managed to open her eyes.

She saw her mother, standing beside her bed, smiling tenderly down at her, just the way Megan remembered from childhood. She was alive and well, and she had come to look after her only daughter.

Megan blinked and strained to keep her eyes open, struggling to keep that beloved face in sight.

'Mam,' she said, and tried to sit up. There were so many questions she wanted to ask, so many things she wanted to say, and to hear. She had never expected to have this chance to talk to her mother again.

'Sleep,' said her mother, and patted her hand. 'Sleep, now, Megan my darling. Everything is going to be all right.'

But everything wasn't all right.

After she came round, Charlie drove Megan home. She had implied to Ted that she could get home under her own steam and that it would be silly for him to take time off work to wait around to pick her up. The truth was she didn't want him to see her in a foggy, post-operative stage. It would worry him; he would agonize and fuss around, not helping but wanting to, and in general simply make things harder for her. All she wanted to do was to get home and sleep it off, and be her normal self again as quickly as possible.

Charlie was a nurse . Unlike Ted, he knew what was needed, and he wasn't personally involved. He knew how to give help so that it could be accepted, without being intrusive or insensitive. He didn't offer her unwanted sympathy, either, and she was grateful for that. He turned the radio on so she didn't even feel she had to make conversation, and he drove her swiftly home, helped her up to bed, and then left.

She was ready and able to go back to work the following night, and able to fend off enquiries about her health with brisk assurance.

Her wish that she wouldn't have to wait long to learn the results of the biopsy was granted when she got a phone call at home two days later from the specialist's office.

'Would you like to make an appointment to come in and talk to Dr Baldwin?'

'So he's had the results?'

'Yes, I believe that's what he wants to talk to you about,' said the receptionist.

Megan made a face, unseen by anyone. She knew the receptionist knew perfectly well – she probably had Megan's file open on the desk before her.

'What are they?'

'Doctor will tell you that himself when you come in.'

'Why don't you make it easier for all of us, and just tell me now?'

'Now, Mrs Roach, you know we're not allowed to give results over the telephone.'

'Oh, for heaven's sake! I'm not your average ignorant patient, you know – I happen to be a nurse! Just give me the results.'

'You'll have to take that up with Dr Baldwin, Mrs Roach. Now, could I put you down for nine o'clock tomorrow morning?'

'Yes,' said Megan, giving in. 'Yes, that would fine.' She hung up the phone, feeling as if a cold hand had touched her heart. She knew that results were not given to patients over the telephone – she knew the rules. But she also knew that rules were made to be broken – when the news was good.

Relatives coming into Casualty with enquiries didn't have to wait for a doctor to tell them that particular patient was out of danger. Good news could be passed on by anyone. It was bad news that was hedged about with ritual and appointment presided over by someone of the proper rank.

The biopsy hadn't solved her problem, that much was clear. She wouldn't know the extent of it until she saw Dr Baldwin. Megan realized that she didn't want to know. She wished she could turn her back on the knowledge, run away from it. But it was too late, and there was nowhere to run.

Standing there on the upstairs landing of her house beside the telephone, Megan closed her eyes and wished for her mother.

# Chapter Six

Megan Moore spent the whole of her ninth summer practising all sorts of strange, physical contortions in an effort to kiss her elbow, having heard that this was a sure way of changing sex.

If only she could turn herself into a boy, she thought, life would be so much better.

It was rotten luck, having been born a girl. She envied her brothers their freedom, which was certain to increase as they grew up. Becoming a woman did not appeal to her at all. The other girls she knew all dreamed of wearing pretty clothes and make-up, of having a husband, and children, and a fine house, but Megan longed for adventure. She liked climbing trees and exploring, and playing games with her brothers – the wilder the better. She was forever in trouble with the nuns at school. She couldn't sit still or keep her clothes tidy to save her soul, it seemed. She was bright, but she was wilful. She wouldn't mind her elders and betters.

'It's her mother's fault,' murmured the nuns, and the neighbours, and her various aunts and cousins when they thought Megan was out of ear-shot. 'The woman lets her daughter run wild.'

Hearing this, Megan burned with anger. But when she leaped to her mother's defence, she only found herself in more trouble – and they were smug and satisfied, as if she just proved them right.

'Oh, leave her be,' her mother would say to those who tried to control her wild daughter.

'Let her have her fun – let her enjoy herself while she may. She'll have sorrows enough when she's older. She'll do a woman's work when she's a woman. She's a girl now, she's a child, she's free: let her be.'

Megan adored her mother. She admired her as well, and pitied her, for Caithleen O'Neil Moore was always too busy looking after her children, her husband, her animals, her house and her garden to go climbing trees and having adventures in the countryside the way her daughter did. When she said she didn't mind, that she really didn't want to climb to the very top of the oldest apple tree in the orchard, Megan couldn't quite believe her. She thought her mother must miss the freedom that Megan now had, and it made her more determined than ever not to grow up and become a woman.

Caithleen listened gravely when Megan confided her plans. 'And if you don't manage to kiss your elbow?'

'I shall – I know I shall! I shall try and try until I do it, no matter how long it takes!'

Caithleen nodded, continuing to shell peas. Her hands were never still. 'If anyone can do it, you can, my love. But, you know, I've never heard of anyone who managed to change from girl to boy, or from boy to girl . . . have you?'

Megan shook her head sadly. She'd been trying not to think about that, concentrating on the task to be done instead of questioning whether the results would be what she hoped for.

'Well, I don't know,' said Caithleen. 'I don't say it is so – there are many strange things in this big, strange world – but it might just be impossible, like a cat turning into a dog.'

Megan stared gloomily at the big blue and white bowl, and ate a pea. 'You mean, I have to be a girl forever?'

'Oh, no, not at all. You're a girl now – and one day you'll be a woman.'

'Oh, yuck!' cried Megan, in real distress.

Caithleen stopped her work and looked down at her daughter. 'I'm a woman, my darling. And I'm happy, I promise you. Does my life seem so dreadful to you?'

In truth, it did seem dreadful, unbearably so. And yet Megan believed her mother when she said she was happy. She just didn't understand how both these things could be.

Megan said, 'You never have time to climb trees or play games . . . even in the evening, you're so tired.

There are so many things you have to do, that you can't do the most fun things. I don't want to stop playing and always take care of other people.'

'I really don't miss climbing trees,' Caithleen said. 'And I love gardening, I love cooking, I love taking care of all of you. Those things are to me as playing is to you. I wouldn't want anything different. Do you believe me?'

Megan nodded. 'But I'm not like you. You're different.'

'Not so very different as you imagine. I was very like you, as a girl. I loved to climb trees – my favourite game was pirates . . . I'd swarm up to the top of the rigging and keep a sharp look-out for other ships . . . and then take my sisters prisoner, and clap them in irons if they misbehaved!'

'When did you stop playing pirates? Did they make you stop, when you got older? Did Dadda make you stop?'

'No, your father didn't make me stop . . . I'd stopped of my own accord before I ever met him. It wasn't so much fun anymore – I had other interests. I was growing up. We like different things when we grow up. I'll bet your father liked to climb trees when he was a boy – why do you suppose he doesn't climb trees anymore? No one ever told him he mustn't. Boys grow up too, you see, it isn't only girls who have to put aside childish things.'

'Oh, yes,' Megan said gloomily. 'The nuns talk

about that . . . Responsibility. Well, I don't want to –
I don't want to grow up!'

'Like it or not, there's not much choice, my love.
Listen, do you remember your favourite game when
you were a baby?'

Warily, Megan shook her head.

'Peek-a-boo!' Caithleen held her hands in front of
her face and then parted them, making a face of surprise as she said the childish words.

Megan blushed and looked at the floor.

'We played it for hours. You could never get
enough of it . . . and now you never play it. You don't
miss playing peek-a-boo with me, do you?'

'Of course not!' Megan exclaimed indignantly.
'That's a baby game!'

'It's a game for babies, and you're a big girl now,
that's right. And when you're a woman, when
you're eighteen, say, or twenty, I'll warrant you
won't miss climbing trees. And responsibility . . . it's
not the grim duty that you seem to think, that the
nuns may make it seem. Not when it grows out of
love. Then it's a pleasure.'

Caithleen looked at her stubborn, disbelieving
daughter, and embraced her. 'Oh, my darling, you
don't understand. But you will some day; you will
be a woman, and glad of it.'

Thirty-four years later Megan Roach sat at her
kitchen table, a cup of tea gone cold by her hand,
and gazed through the window out at her rain-

swept garden. There was one tree in the garden, and she focused on that. It wasn't a good climbing tree, although David, Bernard and Tom had all been up its branches more than once throughout their childhoods. It must have been a good five years or more since that tree had a boy in its branches, she thought. To her knowledge, no girl had ever climbed it, unless she herself could count as a girl when, in her late twenties, she climbed up to rescue a stray kitten for her weeping sons. It would never have occurred to her to climb it for her own pleasure. Her mother had been right, of course, about how she would change. But Megan had known that herself for a very long time.

Megan had grown up very suddenly. Overnight, circumstances had changed her from a twelve-year-old child, still very much a tomboy, to a responsible, twelve-year-old woman.

Puberty came some six months later, and was an anticlimax, not at all the traumatic experience it was for many girls. It merely confirmed, physically, a womanhood which she had already accepted.

Caithleen Moore's death had been sudden and unexpected. No one – except, perhaps, Caithleen, who was not given to complaining about any aches and pains she might have – had even suspected that she might be ill until her appendix ruptured.

Even recognizing the urgency, it took time to get a doctor, and by the time he had managed to drive

Caithleen the many long miles to the nearest hospital, she was past saving.

No one mentioned responsibility to Megan, or told her what she ought to do. She simply took over her mother's role, as far as she could. Meals had to be cooked, laundry had to be done, the house had to be kept clean, her brothers and father needed looking after – Megan responded from the heart, trying to do what her mother would have done. And she discovered that comforting and caring for others helped with her own grief. She was too busy – and too tired after each long day – to brood about what she had lost. And by doing things for her father, and taking care of her brothers, Megan knew that she was doing what Caithleen would have wanted, and so, in a way, she was doing something for Caithleen. She could almost imagine her mother in Heaven, looking down approvingly on her daughter. Because of that, she didn't feel quite so alone. And she didn't blame anyone, or feel resentful about having so suddenly to assume an adult role, a woman's responsibilities. It was inevitable, and it was what she wanted. She couldn't be a child anymore, with her mother dead.

Four years later, Megan's father remarried.

Everyone seemed to think it was a good thing, and appropriate, and approved the match (with a woman ten years his junior), but Megan bitterly resented the interloper. Not for her mother's sake – her father was still in his forties, and Megan didn't expect him to be faithful to her mother's memory to death – but for her own. With a wife, her father had no need of the housekeeper Megan had been. Megan felt displaced.

She should be pleased, they told her. Now she could have a normal adolescence, could have time to herself, could go out with boys . . .

But Megan was no more interested in the normal, trivial adolescent pursuits than she was now in climbing trees or playing peek-a-boo.

A very tense and uneasy year followed her father's marriage. Megan began to think she would have to marry someone, anyone, just to get out of the house – just to have her own house again.

When her brother Neil began to talk about going over the water to England, Megan glimpsed another possible way out.

Neil was musical, with a lovely voice and the ability to play the guitar. His talents weren't entirely appreciated at home, however, because he had a passion for pop music. One of his friends was going to Liverpool, and he wanted Neil to come too. Neil's friend wrote songs, and they both talked vaguely and grandly about starting a band and becoming famous. For some reason, which Megan didn't understand at the time, they seemed to think that getting to Liverpool was the important thing – they would be discovered there, and fame would follow naturally.

Everyone thought Neil was mad, and said so. Except for Megan. Although she was not convinced by his dreams of glory, she backed up his wish to go to England. On one condition: that she go with him. She told her father that she would look after Neil, and keep him out of trouble, as well as keeping house for him and making sure he ate regular meals.

Neil wasn't so keen about being accompanied by his sister, but when he realized that the choice was between going with Megan or not at all, he changed his mind.

So Neil, Neil's friend Kevin O'Donnel, and Megan set off to seek their fortune in England in 1962.

They didn't go to Liverpool, though. They went to Holby, because Kevin had a cousin who owned a house in Holby which he was willing to let them live in for free, so long as they kept the place up and did a bit of decorating.

Holby or Liverpool – by that time it didn't seem to make much difference. Both were in England, both were cities, yet less intimidating than London, both had coffee bars and clubs, both offered potential employment, potential fame . . .

So they thought.

Keeping house for two young men in a big city which offered such heady delights as take-away meals was much less work than looking after a family, house and garden in rural Ireland. Megan liked to keep busy, and she needed a way of earning her living. She had experience in nothing except house-keeping, and she didn't really want to do that. She liked helping people – she was looking for more than just a pay cheque.

Nursing was the obvious choice. She might almost have been born for it.

In later years, when people asked her what had made her decide to become a nurse, Megan found it hard to say. She could remember no surge of enlightenment, no moment of decision. It had just come along, and seemed the right thing to do. She had not planned it, but in retrospect it seemed inevitable.

Was her whole life inevitable? Had it all been planned out by some great force, by Fate, or by the God she still believed in? Had even her cancer been planned, inescapable?

Morbid thoughts. Megan frowned at herself, and stood up. There must be something else she could be doing, something positive, something firmly in the present. Why brood about the past?

She looked at the clock above the cooker. She'd better do something about the boys' supper before she went to work.

'Tom,' she called. 'Tom!'

He was wearing those headphones again, like Ewart Plimmer. Only the music was different. Ewart claimed they didn't cut out sound, and that he could hear perfectly well with them on, but Megan knew otherwise. As usual, she had to practically shout in her youngest son's face before she got his attention, and then he was reluctant to emerge from his cocoon of music.

'If you don't come out, you won't get any supper,' she said, exasperated. 'Now, where's your brother Bernard? If the two of you can agree on what you want to eat, life will be much simpler.'

'Bernard's gone out,' said Tom. 'He won't be eating in. He never does, the first Thursday.'

'First Thursday?'

'It's his science fiction club. That's when they meet. First Thursday of every month, down some pub talking about space ships.'

'Oh,' said Megan blankly. 'Well, do you know if Dave is eating in tonight?'

'Shouldn't think so. He's probably going to be with Anabel.'

'Well, then, it's up to you. What would you like to eat? Whatever you heart desires.'

'Doesn't matter.'

'Humour me.'

'Welllll . . .' he rolled his eyes up, considering. 'I think . . . chips.'

'Chips. Is that all? Is that the best you can do?'

'It's my favourite food.'

'You don't need me to make you chips – you can get a bag of them down the road.'

'You don't want to cook for me? OK, I'll get a take-away.' He moved to put his headphones back on.

70

She stopped him. 'Please, Tom. I do want to cook for you. That's why I'm asking what you want.'

'Well, I told you, didn't I? I like chips . . . and baked beans on toast. Maybe a fried egg with it, or a bit of bacon. Doesn't really matter, as long as there's chips with it. Lots of chips.'

'Oh, all right,' she said, resigned. She had asked for it, after all. But all the foods he had asked for were things he could just as easily eat out, or make for himself. She wanted to do something special for him . . . do something he couldn't do himself. But he didn't want that from her. She felt sad, and she didn't really know why. She went back to the kitchen and began peeling potatoes.

# Chapter Seven

Christopher Baldwin was a tall, thin man in his forties, with carefully-combed, thinning brown hair, wearing an obviously expensive suit with an old school tie. He was looking at some papers, seemingly too busy to look up, when Megan entered his office.

She disliked him immediately.

'Ah, Mrs Roach,' he said in a distracted voice. 'Please, sit down.'

She took the chair beside his desk. She said nothing. He let her sit in silence for a few seconds, then looked directly at her. His eyes – brilliantly blue and fringed with thick, dark lashes – must have made him a hit with the ladies, but she wasn't buying what he was trying to sell.

He smiled at her. 'So, you're part of Plimmer's little army. I've heard a lot about you.'

'Have you indeed?'

'Yes, and from what I hear, the DHSS is not entirely happy about this particular experiment . . . although I'm sure the city would be sorry to see you go.'

'Is anything I say likely to be taken down and used in evidence against me?'

He blinked, disconcerted. 'Sorry?'

'I wasn't aware that you'd asked me here to talk about my work.'

'I was only –'

'Making polite conversation, I know. Save it. Give me the results of the biopsy.'

There were lines like a parenthesis around his thin-lipped mouth. Megan realized she had made Baldwin angry, and she cursed herself for her reckless temper. She knew from experience that most doctors were not above punishing patients who weren't sufficiently respectful. She would have to remember that with this man she wasn't a fellow professional – she was simply another patient.

'You can probably guess,' he said coldly. 'The smear indicated carcinoma in situ, and the biopsy has confirmed this. It has also shown that the carcinoma is more advanced than we had hoped. It has become invasive. It is impossible to tell at this point just how far it might have infected the uterus – or other organs – but there is only one course open to us.'

She wondered if he expected her to supply the answer. She felt as if someone had injected ice-cold water into her veins. She was too cold even to shiver.

More gently now, Baldwin said, 'Cervical cancer has an excellent treatment rate, you know, Mrs Roach. Depending on what we find when we remove the uterus, radiotherapy may not even be necessary. You are likely to be one of the 80 per cent for whom hysterectomy will be a complete cure.'

'So that's it? You take out my womb, and, bingo, I'm well again? A miracle cure!'

Megan could tell he didn't like her tone. She wasn't being sufficiently grateful – and not at all respectful.

'That is what we hope, Mrs Roach. There is always the chance that we could be wrong, and that the carcinoma has already infiltrated . . . but this sort of speculation is fruitless. Why not look on the bright side? You should be grateful that your problem is one that can be dealt with relatively easily.'

Megan stared at the doctor in open, mocking disbelief. 'Oh, I'm to be grateful, am I? Grateful for my cancer! Well, that's a new one! Tell me, Dr Baldwin, did you ever consider that you might have a vocation for the priesthood?'

He flushed angrily. 'Mrs Roach. I can understand your distress, believe me. But you are not making a difficult situation any easier. I am simply trying to present the case to you as clearly as I can, and you –'

'And I am insufficiently grateful. Yes, I do realize that, doctor. Perhaps I'll change my mind when I've had some time to think about it, but just now I find it difficult to be thankful that I am about to lose my womb.'

'It's not an organ you have any use for,' he said brutally. 'Admit it. You're forty-five –'

'Forty-three,' she corrected, her vanity absurdly stung.

74

He nodded, accepting the correction, looking down at her file. 'You have three children, the last one born seventeen years ago . . . obviously, you made up your mind a long time ago that three was enough. And even if you hadn't decided, nature has decided for you; you are menopausal. You're never going to have any more children. Your uterus is useless to you now. More than that, it's a danger to your life.'

'You've made your point, Dr Baldwin.'

'You're a nurse, Mrs Roach. You should be able to look at this practically. I recommend you don't start getting sentimental about your identity as a woman . . . it will only make things much harder for you.'

He paused as if waiting for her reply, but Megan said nothing. She could think of nothing to say.

Baldwin nodded, satisfied. He reached for a desk diary. 'There's no sense putting it off. I think I can manage to get a bed for you in the next couple of weeks . . . let's see . . .'

'Wait. Not yet. I . . . I'll have to think about it first.'

He frowned, then looked knowing. 'Would you like me to talk to your husband, Mrs Roach?'

'Certainly not!' Her heart lurched unpleasantly at the image of Christopher Baldwin taking Ted aside for a little man-to-man talk. 'I can tell him myself.'

'I only meant . . . I simply thought that you might find it easier if I explained it to him. Explained what it meant. If he had some idea that . . . I can assure you that the removal of the uterus need not affect your, er, marital relations at all.'

'I've tended hysterectomy patients,' Megan said. 'I know what they go through . . . we're talking about major surgery here, not some little snipping and tying of tubes . . . I know how long it can take to recover.' She sighed, and then looked directly at Baldwin, asking with her eyes for some understanding. 'All I'm asking is a little time to think about it . . . I'm not looking for a way out. I just want to try to come to terms with it before you set the date. That's all.'

She couldn't tell whether or not she had made any impression on him. Baldwin simply looked at her, unmoving. 'Don't take too long,' was all he said.

Megan was rushed off her feet that night at work, and glad of it. Although she had asked Dr Baldwin for time to think, thinking was the last thing she felt like doing.

She knew Baldwin was right. It had nothing to do with liking him or not – any doctor would have given her the same diagnosis. She would have the hysterectomy. Lose her womb – useless to her now, anyway – and live to a ripe old age, instead of dying of cancer before she was fifty. It was the right thing to do, and no amount of thinking would either change that or make it easier for her. By putting it off, by asking for time, she was just trying to run away.

When Ted met her at the end of the shift, Megan slumped in the front seat and closed her eyes, too exhausted both physically and emotionally to speak. She was too wound up to sleep, but she kept her eyes closed until the car stopped.

The sight that met her eyes woke her up immediately. 'What are we doing here?' she asked.

Instead of taking her home, Ted had driven to a small roadside park with a panorama of the scenic Avon Gorge.

As Megan blinked in weary bewilderment, Ted reached behind the seat and brought out a bottle of champagne.

Only then did she remember. 'Today's our anniversary.'

'Since you've got to work tonight, I thought we'd do our celebrating first thing.' He wound down the window and uncorked the bottle. 'Here's to our twenty-third year. May there be many more.'

It was on this very spot – although in a different car – that Ted had proposed to Megan in 1964.

'Put this on,' said Ted.

He was extending a pair of headphones towards her, attached to a small tape player.

Megan regarded it suspiciously. 'Where'd you get that?'

'Borrowed it.'

'If they find out you've nicked it –'

'I didn't nick it! I borrowed it. From me own son. Now will you give a listen?'

She let him fit the headphones, and turn the tape on. It was the Beatles, singing 'A Hard Day's Night'. That was the film Ted and Megan had been to see just before he proposed.

The music went through her head, around and around. She stared at Ted, seeing the man she had been married to for twenty-three years, the father of her children, her other half . . . seeing also, beneath the stubble and the lines on his face, the shy youth he had been when he had proposed. Her first and only love. Now, then, and forever.

The discordant clash of chords jarred in her ears, and Megan burst out crying.

'Now, now, none of that; this was supposed to make you happy, not sad!'

She took the headphones off, still weeping. 'I am happy . . . I am.'

'Funny way you've got of showing it.'

'Oh, Ted, I do love you.'

'Now, now, none of that. We're an old married couple now . . . have some more of this.'

She sipped obediently, sniffed, wiped her eyes and blew her nose. 'I guess I'm tired.'

'And no wonder, the way they work you. I've been thinking. Maybe you should go back to working days.'

'Oh, Ted, I can't. Not now. This isn't just any night job, you know . . . it's a special team, and I'm proud to be a part of it. Plimmer's Army.' She laughed, rue-fully. 'Although how long it will last, I do not know. There was a man from the DHSS doing a spot check a little while ago, and I don't think he went away with a very good impression of us. So they may decide to close us down at any time. But until they do, I'll be there.'

'You ought to think about yourself sometimes, not always other people. You're tired –'

'I'm tired, but it's not the hours,' she said firmly. 'You know I've always found it easy to stay up nights . . . remember when the boys were small?'

'I remember sometimes it seemed you never slept at all. I don't know how you did it.'

'Nor do I.'

'But you're not that young any more. And after so many years – after all your experience – I think you shouldn't have to push yourself so hard. You should be able to take it a little easier. You need a change. Something's wrong – I – I can see there is.'

It was an obvious struggle for Ted to say so much, and Megan appreciated the effort. 'It's not the job. It's not the hours,' she said. 'It's – you know these tests I've been going in for?'

'Change of life, you mean?' asked Ted swiftly. 'Is that what it is? Maybe you should get the doctor to give you some tablets.'

Change of life. Female problems. The perfect, all-purpose excuse. Men didn't want to talk about it . . .

they didn't understand, and didn't expect to. How tempting it was just to leave it at that, to let Ted believe that what was happening to her was natural and normal, something she could take in her stride.

But she had to tell him of course. And there might never be a better time.

Yet, when she opened her mouth, she found herself saying, 'Do you ever feel sorry that we didn't have a daughter?'

Ted looked surprised by the question, but not as surprised as Megan felt. Now where, she wondered, had *that* come from?

'No,' he said. Then he thought about it. 'It would have been nice. I remember when you were pregnant with Tom, I was thinking what a little girl would be like. But now we've got the boys, I can't imagine it any different. Why? Do you feel sorry?'

'I don't know,' she said slowly. 'I know we decided that three was enough . . . but just lately I've been wondering . . . I've been thinking about having another baby.'

The mixture of alarm and bewilderment on Ted's face was almost comical.

'Another baby? Now? You? Me? But – I thought – I didn't think – is it – are you trying to tell me that you're pregnant?'

Suddenly Megan saw the funny side of it. She began to laugh. 'Well, why not? The boys are finally grown up – they don't need me anymore – what else should I do but start all over again? And what an anniversary surprise for you . . . Oh, the very idea! No, no, oh, no, Ted, no. I'm not pregnant; I'll never be pregnant again.'

She laughed until the tears poured down her face. Ted stared at her in ever-deepening bafflement.

Finally the hysteria passed. Finally she stopped laughing. She ached inside. She wiped the tears from her face with the backs of her hands, and gulped down some champagne.

'Sorry, love, I've had a hard day,' she said quietly. 'A hard day's night. I'm not pregnant. I don't know what made me say that just then. Well, maybe I do. I've been thinking about the past. But I'm not pregnant – I'll never be pregnant again. My childbearing days are over. I should have known that after Tom was born but somehow, there was always the possibility. You wouldn't think something called a possibility could be so important, would you? The possibility of life, the possibility of death.

'I'm going to have a hysterectomy, Ted. I saw the doctor today, and he told me. I – God, I can hardly say it! – I have cancer. They think if they take the womb out that will cure it. There's a very good chance it will. So I'm having a hysterectomy. Why not? It's the only thing to do. And not before time.'

Megan leaned back and closed her eyes. 'Take me home, please, love. I'm so tired. Don't say a word. Just take me home.'

# Chapter Eight

Ted and the boys had not been left to fend for themselves since the last time Megan had gone away without them – seventeen years before, when some slight complications after Tom's birth had kept her in hospital for more than a week.

Then, Megan had considered herself lucky to find the house still standing when she came home. Despite some major disasters, the cooker had not exploded, and only two saucepans had been burned beyond saving. But the filth of the place! You'd think Ted had been locked in with two infants and no outside help for months on end, when in fact all Ted had to do was to bath his two sons and put them to bed at night, get them up and dressed in the morning before taking them over the road to Mrs Biggs. At that time Megan had thought that Ted would at least be able to keep himself fed and washed and dressed, and do a few minimal things around the house. She didn't expect tidiness, or even her own high standards of cleanliness, but she could never have imagined the complete degeneration into primitive squalor which took place in the space of about ten days.

Days later she was still finding dirty nappies and evidence of fish and chips stashed away in the most unlikely places.

Since that time, Megan had developed the habit of treating her husband and three sons as if they were utterly helpless to fend for themselves. She expected no more of them than she did of the dogs: she'd give them their meals, and in return, they weren't to bury dead things under the carpets.

But now, although she couldn't expect the dogs to change, Megan was going to have to ask more of the men in her family.

She planned for her departure by cooking masses of pies and casseroles, things which could be frozen and then simply put in the oven to provide a good, hot, nutritious meal with a minimum of fuss. She also drew up balanced menus of meals which were simple to prepare: even Tom could read the instructions and put potatoes in the oven to bake in their jackets and a couple of chops on the grill.

Her best friend Sarah had already promised to drop by every day just to see how 'the boys' were getting along and if anything were needed, and Megan also knew that she could count on the Garnetts next door to lend a hand where it was needed.

'Don't worry about us,' said Ted. 'We'll be all right.'

But Megan went on imagining scenarios and

thinking up ways of coping, as responsible and organized as a general before the big battle.

She had already decided she didn't have to worry
about Dave, who had his Anabel to look after him,
and that gave her another thought.

'If you and Anabel are going to be seeing each
other anyway, maybe instead of you going to her,
she could come to the house and cook for all of you,'
Megan suggested to her eldest son.

Dave grinned. 'Anabel cook! That's not likely,' he
said. 'I had to teach her how to fry an egg.'

'You taught her . . . and where did you learn to fry
an egg, may I ask?'

'Watching you . . . and then trial and error.'

Megan stared at him, baffled, and shook her head.
'Well, I don't know . . . fancy a girl not knowing how
to cook.'

'She didn't want to know how to cook,' Dave said.
'She didn't want to be like her mother, always stuck
in the kitchen when there were so many other things
she was interested in. She's probably right . . . she
can always learn later, if she wants.'

'But you're always over there . . . what do you do
for meals?'

'Take-away, mostly. Sometimes her flat-mate does
a big pot of beans and vegetable curry, or ratatouille.
Sometimes I do bacon and eggs, or we have sandwiches.

'And when you get bored with that, you eat at

home. Ah, well, maybe Anabel's right. If I'd forced you lads to fend for yourselves early on, I wouldn't have to worry that as soon as I go away you'll all die of malnutrition.'

'It takes more than a couple of weeks to die of malnutrition, Mum. I think we're safe.'

Still, worrying about others was a good way of not worrying about herself. And, deep down, where she tried to keep it hidden, Megan was worried about herself.

She didn't have long to wait before going into hospital for the operation. This was something to be grateful for in a time of too few hospital beds, but it was also worrying. It meant she couldn't be shunted off on to a waiting list composed of other 'non-urgent' cases. It meant her case was serious, that waiting was too dangerous. Megan didn't want to think about that.

So, in her usual way, Megan thought about everyone else, instead.

She was still at it as Ted drove her to the hospital, making lists in her mind, going over and over all the things she usually did without thinking about, trying to tell Ted everything he needed to know, a crash course in survival.

It was odd to be going to the hospital in the morning, and odder still to be going in as a patient instead of a worker – but she wasn't going to think about that.

As they drove through the fresh, rain-washed morning Megan said, 'I made a list of all the things that need to be done, and I put a copy of it on the fridge.'

'On the fridge door,' said Ted. 'Right.'

'The TV repairman is coming tomorrow morning, so make sure someone is there to let him in. Bernard should be in – he usually is – but I can't remember if I mentioned it to him. You'd better tell him, just to make sure he doesn't decide to go off to the library or something.

'And the dogs. Don't forget, Oliver likes two handfuls of mix where our Bowson only likes one.'

'What time?'

'I do it about six . . . anyway, I'm sure I put it on the list, and Tom should know everything about the dogs. It's just he forgets the time with that music always pounding in his head . . .' Ted turned the taxi in to the ambulance terminal, and Megan felt the faint, beginning sense of panic. Had she forgotten anything?

'Talking of eating, I've filled the freezer full of food, so make sure you use it. Remember to take something out to defrost every morning.'

'I'll be all right,' Ted said.

'No eating out,' said Megan. She tried for a teasing tone. 'I know you, the first chance you get you'll be down to the chippy.'

'Here, look at that,' said Ted.

The surprise in his voice alerted her. She glanced up, through the windscreen. Her mouth formed into an 'O' of surprise, but for a moment she couldn't speak.

There they were, all her workmates, waiting for her, lined up outside Casualty. A welcoming party. Instead of going home when their shift was over, they had stayed to see her. They were all on hand: Charlie, Baz, Susie, Duffy, Plimmer, King, Kuba, Ponting and Mute.

Susie and Duffy were holding bunches of multi-coloured balloons. As Ted stopped the car, Clive King and Kuba began to unfurl the banner they held.

On it, in big letters, had been painted the immortal words: 'DON'T WORRY – YOU'LL JUST FEEL A SMALL PRICK.'

As Megan emerged from the car, everyone began to applaud.

Megan's cheeks were warm. She wasn't used to being the centre of attention, and she wished she could hide. Ted, meanwhile, had got out of the car and was getting her case, acting as if everything was normal, ignoring all the fuss.

She looked at Charlie, who, for some reason, was standing up on a crate in the midst of the welcoming party.

'If this was your idea, Charles Fairhead,' she said, 'you are never going to live it down.'

Charlie looked not at all abashed or frightened.

He might have been one of the loonies at Speaker's Corner in Hyde Park on his make-shift platform as he raised his arms and launched into his speech.

'Ladies and gentlemen. We are gathered here, in the sight of Holby City Hospital, to welcome the multi-talented Megan Roach to the delights of institutionalized cooking, bedsocks and the old favourite, the bunch of grapes. Your hands, please.'

Everyone burst into renewed applause, and Clive stepped forward to present Megan with a huge bunch of purple grapes, and a rather smaller bouquet of red, white and yellow carnations. Baz also came forward with some beautiful irises.

Megan hardly knew which way to look. 'Ted, give us a hand with these,' she said. Then she turned back to the smiling, concerned and friendly faces of the people she worked with night after night and said with a mock-scowl, 'And you lot can move yourselves right now before I start blushing!'

Laughing, reluctant, they began to disperse.

Ewart Plimmer emerged from the crowd. 'Sorry about the banner,' he said.

Megan looked at it again, and couldn't help smiling. 'Yeah, it's not a very original gag, is it?'

Baz pressed her arm. 'I'll pop up tonight,' she said.

Megan shook her head. 'You'll be lucky if you have five minutes to yourself – never mind about coming up to see me.'

'There's always time for the important things,'

said Baz, moving away.

'I'll come and help you eat those grapes,' Clive said with a grin.

'See you later, Megan,' said Charlie, going off after Baz. He mimed ducking a blow.

Megan simply shook her head, again unable entirely to repress a smile.

'Megan,' said Ted.

She looked at him and felt her stomach clench in sympathy at the fear she saw behind his eyes. She couldn't help him with that fear – she couldn't take it away or deny it because she felt it, too.

'You shoot off now,' she said briskly, as if she were just leaving for a day's work.

'You sure you don't want me to . . .'

'No,' she said firmly. Then, more gently. 'No, go on now, love – scram. I know my way from here.'

'I'll give you a hand with these,' said Duffy, taking the flowers and grapes from her.

Megan and Ted looked at each other for a long moment. Then they kissed, and Ted got into the car. But he was still reluctant to leave, still too worried to drive away.

'Look,' he said. 'If you need anything . . . whatever . . . anything you forgot, or, you know . . . anything at all, just let me know, and I'll bring it right in. OK?'

'Sounds like this is my moment to plump for a fur coat,' said Megan. 'Lucky for you I've never wanted a fur.' She made a face. 'Go on, now! Anyone would think I was in for life the way you lot are jazzing about. Just move.'

'Well,' said Ted awkwardly. 'See you, then.'

She planted another quick kiss on the side of his face. 'Don't forget to look at the list on the fridge door, and do what it says!'

Megan turned to Duffy as Ted drove off and said, low-voiced, 'Hates hospitals. Scares the pants off him. Right. In we go.'

Some of the others were still waiting, clustered around the door. Megan smiled at them awkwardly, feeling that something was called for, but not knowing what.

'You're all a bunch of loonies,' she said. 'And I'm very grateful. Now go to bed.'

Kuba launched dramatically into song. 'We'll meet again . . . oof!'

Without looking around, Megan knew that Susie had belted him one. She chuckled appreciatively, and met Duffy's eye.

A moment later the two nurses were laughing uproariously as they entered the hospital.

# Chapter Nine

Megan was well-used to sleeping during the day, and she had her earplugs to shut out the sounds of the surgical ward, but she only managed the occasional cat-nap that first day in hospital. She was too aware that she was not at home in her own bed . . . too aware of where she was, what she was waiting for and why.

She had brought along some magazines to read. She had even told herself that she would be glad to have the time, for once, to read an entire issue through in the month it was published, instead of snatching bits and pieces in rare moments of spare time, so that she read Christmas recipes in August and finished the Special Bumper Summer Fiction Special sometime after Christmas.

But now that she had the time, her attention wandered. And there was something about this issue which was less appealing than usual. There was an article about the life of a nurse – how little money they made, and how much dedication and time was expected of them in return. One nurse was quoted as saying she would not leave her profession, but she would have to leave London because she couldn't afford to live there any longer. Her younger sister, who worked in an estate agent's office, owned a car and had just bought a flat with her boyfriend, whereas the nurse shared a three-room rented flat with two other nurses and went everywhere by bike, unable even to afford public transport.

'So what else is new?' murmured Megan. Even after years of experience, nursing was not a well-paid profession.

But no one went into nursing to make money, and that, she thought, was as it should be. A sense of dedication was important in nurses as well as teachers – no one should be drawn to it by the thought of getting rich.

And yet, she thought now, there was something seriously wrong in a society which rewarded someone who answered the telephone, typed up house descriptions, and took people on tours of outrageously over-priced properties more highly than someone who saved people's lives. Even though she believed that nursing was and always should remain a vocation rather than a career in the usual sense, it wasn't fair to ask people to sacrifice themselves to it, to give up all hope of a modestly comfortable life for the sheer joy of knowing that what they did made a difference in the world, and improved other people's lives.

Even leaving fairness aside, it just didn't make

sense. If she had it to do all over again, even knowing what she knew now, Megan thought she would still choose nursing. But if Ted had died and left her to bring the boys up alone? If that had happened – or if Ted had been out of work – and she'd been offered a better-paying job, Megan knew she would have had to take it. She might have been willing to sacrifice her own comfort for pride in her work, but not if Ted or the boys had needed something else.

Megan put the magazine aside when she realized she had been staring at the same page for fifteen minutes without taking in a word of it. She needed some escapism, she thought, and reached for the book Anabel had given her.

It touched her that Anabel had gone to the trouble of getting her a present, even though it was a book she found slightly intimidating. She wasn't much of a reader, and hadn't often picked up a book since the days when the boys needed her help with their school-work.

*The Color Purple* it was called. By Alice Walker. According to the cover, there had been a film made of it, but the title didn't register with Megan. She wondered why Anabel had chosen this particular book. Had she tried to pick something she thought would especially appeal to Megan, or was it one of her own favourites?

The book was written in an unusual style, and although she was interested in the story, Megan found her attention wandering. Finally she gave up, let her mind wander as it would, and listened to the radio.

Much of the music played by the hospital station was mere background noise to Megan. Occasionally she recognized things that her sons liked, or popular hits of years past, but even in those cases she usually couldn't have pinned a name or a particular year to the song. She knew them, but they didn't mean anything to her. But every once in a while a particular song would touch a chord in her, and like a powerful drug it would release a flood of memories, emotions and sensations from her past.

Early Beatles songs always did that to her – songs like 'She Loves You' and 'Do You Want to Know a Secret' would send her back to the time when she was young, and England a brand new country to her; and back, especially, to the time when she first fell in love with Ted.

Like her brother Neil, Ted Roach was a young man besotted with pop music and dreaming (although a lot more shyly than the ever self-confident Neil) of fame.

Neil and Ted met in a coffee bar and struck up an instant friendship. Neil was the singer, his mate Kevin played lead guitar, and they all decided that Ted would be the drummer – just as soon as he could afford to buy some drums and learn to play them.

Megan smiled fondly and wistfully to herself,

remembering how it had been to be so young that anything seemed possible. How long had Ted gone on dreaming of being a drummer, she wondered? His interest in music had been more of a passing fad; it didn't run as deep as her brother's. Ted never had learned to play the drums. She wondered if he ever regretted that.

By the time of the evening shift, Megan was as far from sleep as ever, and her mood was somewhere between melancholy and mellow. Charlie was her first visitor.

He came rambling in with his casual grin and usual zany remarks, as if this was standard practice and he often dropped in on Megan while she was tucked up in bed. He plopped himself down on the edge of the bed, ready to have a little gossip. He took a chocolate bar out of his pocket and began to unwrap it.

Megan stared at the chocolate bar. Whatever he was saying faded out, and the chocolate expanded to fill the universe.

She shut her eyes, gulped hard, and then opened them again to fix an accusing stare on her unwitting tormentor.

'Charlie Fairhead, I am lying here, nil-by-mouth, and you are stuffing your face with the sexiest-looking bar of chocolate I've ever seen in my life. Would you call that sensitive nursing?'

Charlie froze like a rabbit in front of an on-coming car, then crammed the rest of the chocolate into his mouth. 'Psychology,' he mumbled. He swallowed, and licked his lips. 'So you remember what it's like when you get out of here.' Then he rolled his eyes at his own excuse, hunched his shoulders and treated her to his best hang-dog expression. 'Pig-ignorance,' he confessed.

'That's what I like about you . . . deep down there is an honest, sensitive human being.'

Charlie looked suspicious. 'You taking the micky?'

'No, actually. Changed me mind about you.' She sighed. 'I must be going soft in here.'

He looked around the room, as if seeking the reason, then fixed her with a steady look. 'You've been listening to the hospital radio, haven't you?'

Megan nodded guiltily. 'Worse than that . . . well, almost. Do you know what I nearly did? I nearly requested a tune for Ted.'

'You didn't!'

'No, I didn't. I managed to stop myself just in time. It's terrible, isn't it? There I was, halfway through my fifth ice-cube, and the silly sod of a DJ goes and plays "Tie a Yellow Ribbon Round the Old Oak Tree". I was nearly choking on my pillow.'

' "Tie a Yellow Ribbon"?' he repeated in disbelief.

'Yes, well, say what you like, that song always means to me chips and Ted on the Costa del Sol. Every time I hear it, I'm straight back there, sitting in

the sun, feeling the heat on my bare arms and legs . . .
I can almost smell the vinegar.'

'I think that means you're hungry.'

'Yes, well, you're right about that . . . but oh,
Charlie, I *am* going soft in here. Nothing to do but
think, dream about the past, or worry about the
future. No good trying to sleep. I've been on night
duty too long. Just look at the place . . . dead as a
morgue, and it smells like the ladies – guaranteed to
depress you.'

Charlie squeezed her hand. She could tell he was
listening, not just pretending to be sympathetic, and
suddenly she wanted to talk to him, really talk, as
she had not been able to do for so long. Charlie
was far from being her closest friend – in fact, their
relationship was rather a prickly one, because he
was, in fact, her superior, even though they both recognized that her years of experience, as well as her
own personal store of common sense, gave her the
advantage in everything except rank. Taking orders
from Charlie sometimes felt like being bossed by one
of her sons.

But they weren't at work now, and although he
was close, he wasn't family. She *could* talk to him.
Before she could pause to reconsider, Megan voiced
the words that had been haunting her unsaid.

'I've got cancer. And having a hysterectomy . . .
well, maybe it will cure it, but maybe it won't.
Nobody's saying it, but I know just as well as the

doctors that there's a chance that it's already spread . . . they just don't know. They can hope, but there's a chance it's already too late. I've got cancer, and I can't think about anything else.'

She turned her head away, all at once frightened by her own words, and by the thought of Charlie's sympathy. She didn't want verbal comfort, words she couldn't believe, like putting a plaster on an amputated limb. She told herself she shouldn't have said anything. It was better to keep your fears inside. She didn't want Charlie thinking she was weak, and feeling sorry for her.

'Look,' she said hastily. 'You go on, don't listen to me. I'm getting a bit morbid in here on my own, nobody to think about but myself. I'm all right, really. You go on. I'm sure I'll fall asleep.'

'Listen,' said Charlie, standing up. 'I've just had an idea. You hang on in there, sister . . . I'll be back

'Charlie, it's all right, really –'

He held his hand up to stop her protests. 'No worries,' he said. He was gone before she could stop him or say anything else.

'Charlie,' she said, to the empty room.

It was Charlie who had thought up the little arrival party that morning, and now he had thought of something else to make life a little more interesting – not only for Megan, but for the whole team.

He found King in the administration area, filling

out blood samples, and told him his plan.

King gave him a look, unimpressed.

'This is a mercy mission, my son,' said Charlie.

'What's to stop you ringing the Night Sister and asking if you can bring her down?'

Charlie had already thought of that. After all, Megan was neither in pain nor infectious, and there was no reason why, since she was already awake, she shouldn't join her mates downstairs. There was no reason why she should have to lie about in her uncomfortable hospital bed, bored out of her mind and worried half to death when night shift in Casualty offered so many fine distractions.

No reason at all, except for rules. And although to Charlie rules were only made to be broken, not everyone felt the same way. As he had learned to his cost.

He leaned closer to King. 'You want to ring Sister Phillips and ask?'

'Come again?'

Charlie made his face mask-like and unforgiving. 'Sister Brunhilde.'

King nodded, understanding. He put the last of the blood samples away. 'Give me ten minutes.'

'Good man,' said Charlie. Then, remembering his duty, 'Get Duffy to fast bleep us if it gets busy.'

'Right. At least it's not a Saturday night.'

Charlie went off in search of Kuba.

Megan was still wide awake, gazing blankly at her

flowers and resisting the lure of the radio, when Charlie returned. She was somewhat nonplussed to see Kuba right behind Charlie – with a wheelchair.

'Megan!' exclaimed Kuba joyously. 'We have come to rescue you!'

'Rescue me? Charlie, I think this is your doing.'

Charlie bowed. 'We have come to rescue you indeed, from the twin dragons of this ward – boredom, and Sister Philips.'

Megan smothered a laugh. 'But . . .'

'But me no buts, Mrs Roach. We're going to take you down to Casualty, where you can see all your friends . . . much more fun for you than sitting up here all on your tod, and easier for us if we don't have to keep nipping up here to visit you. If Mohammed cannot come to the mountain, you see, the mountain will . . . er . . .'

'Comparing me to a mountain, are you Charlie? Very flattering, I'm sure!'

'You are not like a mountain!' Kuba protested. 'You are a very good size for a woman – very much appreciated in my country.'

'Thank you, Kuba,' Megan sighed.

'Into the wheelchair, please, madam,' said Charlie.

Megan swung her legs over the edge of the bed and found her slippers. 'I'm perfectly able to walk, you know.'

'I know, but there are certain rules in a hospital, Mrs Roach.'

'Most of which you seem to break as a matter of principle!'

Charlie clutched his heart. 'Oh, to be so cruelly misunderstood! Get in the wheelchair. We can't have you walking out of here under your own steam. This way, if we get caught, you've been abducted by us, and it's not your fault. I'll take all the blame.'

'Ah, Charlie, what a gentleman you are,' Megan said, allowing Kuba to help her into the wheelchair. 'How are we going to get past Sister Philips?'

'Oh, King's arranged a diversion. I think he's going to dazzle her with some fancy footwork while we sneak past, just out of her line of sight.'

'Why do I think this is not going to work?'

And yet it did. While King kept Sister Philips engaged in conversation, blocking her view of the corridor, Kuba and Charlie spirited Megan away, at one point zooming her down the corridor so fast that she clutched the arms of her chair and grinned like a kid playing at racing cars. In no time at all, they had her in the lift, and soon arrived triumphant in the staffroom.

Kuba and Charlie shook hands with each other, and then with Megan. They all beamed idiotically as if they'd won a race.

Then their smiles faded. Charlie picked up a stack of admission cards to see what work was waiting for him.

'I better go,' said Kuba. 'I see you soon, Megan, OK?' Looking vaguely guilty, he left the room.

Megan stared at Charlie. 'Now what?'

'Now you just sit tight, relax, enjoy yourself . . .'

'Enjoy myself, right, when I'm not even allowed a cup of tea!'

'I'll fix you one if you like.'

'Charlie!'

'Aw, come on, Megan. I was only trying to help. Surely this is better than lying up there in that morgue – that's what you called it yourself – waiting for morning. If you can't sleep here, it doesn't matter. At least you'll have company.'

'Yeah, sure. Enough's enough, Charlie. It was a good joke, but now you'd better take me back.'

'But you've only just arrived! And the others would never forgive me if they didn't have a chance to see you while you're here.'

Not for the first time, Megan felt as if she was arguing with one of her sons. 'You know all hell is going to break loose if Ewart finds me here. Now come on, Charlie.'

'He doesn't need to know, does he? Anyway, he's up to here in paperwork tonight . . . probably won't even come out of his office.'

The door to the staffroom swung open. Megan tensed, certain it would be Ewart. But it was Duffy, who stared at her in pleased surprise.

'Megan! What are you doing here?'

Megan canted her head in Charlie's direction. 'All his idea – I'm supposed to relax in the company of

102

my colleagues while Sister Philips and the rest of the hospital haven't a clue as to where I am.' She threw Charlie a challenging look. 'What was it you called it again, this great idea of yours?'

'Team therapy.' He smiled charmingly.

'Kidnapped, more like,' said Megan. 'Oh, I shouldn't complain. I asked for it. I was bored to death up there, and would have walked out on me own if I'd dared . . . only Sister Philips is hovering over my head like Beelzebub and the seven black devils all rolled into one, which makes relaxing just a wee bit difficult.'

Duffy filled the kettle and began to make a pot of tea. 'So how did you wangle it, this great escape?'

'A carefully rehearsed decoy and meticulous planning,' said Charlie.

'It's a wonder we didn't wake the whole hospital, the noise you were making,' said Megan.

'We were brilliant!'

King stuck his head into the room. 'Charlie, we got a kid on the way, unconscious.'

Charlie responded at once. 'What?'

'Query OD, query alcohol,' said King.

'Tea, Megan?'

Megan looked around at Duffy, and then did a double-take. The younger nurse was wearing a Spiderman hood. 'Where did that come from?'

'I know what it is,' said Charlie, pausing in the doorway just long enough to appreciate Duffy's disguise. 'You've had your hair done.'

The three of them went out, leaving Megan alone.

Megan sighed, looked wistfully at the steaming teapot, then folded her hands in her lap and shook her head. 'Well, here we are again,' she said aloud.

King came back about half an hour later. 'Tea, Megan?'

'Nil-by-mouth . . . but don't let me stop you. You sip, I'll watch. What's happening?'

He shook his head. 'What isn't?'

'Spiderman?'

'Oh, he'll live. Couple of broken bones, that's all.'

'What?'

King looked at her, realized she didn't know anything about it and laughed. 'Yeah, we had Spiderman in tonight . . . some bloke who likes to get dressed up and then climb in through the bedroom window to give his wife a thrill, only this time, I guess his super spider-powers failed him, 'cause he fell off the wall.'

'I'm sorry I missed it.'

King blew on his tea.

'Where's Kuba?' Megan asked. 'I haven't seen him since the great escape . . . I thought he'd be keeping me company.'

'He's probably lying low, trying to keep out of Plimmer's way.'

'Why? Not because of me?'

'No, no. Because of me. I said if he didn't tell Plimmer, I would. His latest crazy idea. A raffle. He

104

must have told you about it. Going around selling tickets to the patients . . . like hot cakes, he said. I'll bet! Who would dare not buy a ticket if Kuba wanted to sell them one?'

Baz came in, moving like a zombie, and slumped into a chair. Megan gave her a sympathetic glance, but said nothing.

King went on, 'He claims he's made fifteen pounds already. How's he going to give that back?'

'He can't,' said Megan. 'Maybe he should put it in the blind box.'

'Course, now he's wandering around like a lost saint trying to find his halo. And the way he's been looking at me –'

Baz roused herself. 'Who are you talking about?'

'Kuba,' said King. 'He organized a raffle to raise money for a ventilator.'

'Oh, how sweet,' said Baz.

'I agree,' said Megan. 'And if you high-principled men had stopped fussing, he probably could have carried on without a hitch.'

'Yeah, but it's against the rules,' said King.

'Ah, sod the rules! Where's your sense of spontaneity? I mean, it's not as if he's running around pulling his trousers down every five minutes . . .'

'What the hell's that got to do with it?'

Megan looked at Baz, who also looked baffled. Slightly thrown now, Megan nevertheless battled on. 'Well, you know what I mean, he's not doing any harm, in fact, he's trying to do good, and maybe if you let him . . . Sometimes I think you're really unfair to Kuba. You lot treat him as if he's a member of some sub-normal species, from time to time.'

'Rubbish,' said King. 'He just behaves like an ass sometimes.'

'We all do,' said Megan.

King sighed, and then smiled slightly, accepting. 'OK.' He put his teacup down. 'Let's call a truce.'

'Truce,' Megan agreed.

When King had gone, she looked at Baz and smiled, 'You know, I could really get into this – the wise old woman – I feel like Mother Teresa, sitting here, dishing out the morals.'

'Don't get into it too much – we need you out there.'

'Bad night?'

'Bloody awful. Full of people hiding things or mis-understanding things.'

'Sounds familiar.'

'You see, that's what I miss when you're not there – the Megan Roach approach.'

They both laughed.

There was the sound of a commotion outside, and they looked at each other, not shocked, but waiting.

'Probably just a wino,' said Megan.

'Pub falling-out time,' said Baz.

The commotion grew louder. A woman was screaming in Gujerati and wailing.

'I'd better go and check on it,' said Baz.

'I'll be here, if you need any advice,' Megan said, only half-joking.

'I may take you up on that.'

'Anytime, Baz.'

Megan was not alone for long. Within a few minutes of Baz leaving, Ewart Plimmer entered with a young woman. It took Megan a moment to realize that this was his daughter.

'Oh, hello, Ewart,' Megan said.

She saw the surprise flicker across his face, but he quickly masked it. 'I'm glad to see you've not lost touch, Megan. You know my daughter, Gillian? She just dropped in for a chat, only I'm a bit tied up for the moment, so I thought she could wait in here . . . if you don't mind?'

'Of course. Hello Gillian. Make yourself at home.'

Gillian gave Megan a wary, awkward look. 'Thanks.'

'Right,' said Ewart. 'I'll leave you two together. Shouldn't be long.'

Megan did not break the silence which fell when Ewart shut the door. She had last seen Gillian when the girl was recovering from the effects of too much alcohol – Megan had been the first to deal with her, and to recognize her when she refused to give her name, when she had been brought into Casualty.

Finally Gillian looked full at Megan, and asked quietly, 'Were you the one who cleaned me up when

I was brought in?'

Megan nodded. 'Yes.' Then she said in a confessional tone, 'I'm not supposed to be here at all, you know. Thought I was in trouble when your old man came in. I'm in for an operation, and I should be upstairs in the ward tucked up in bed like a good girl. But you know what they say about doctors and nurses . . .'

Gillian smiled.

'Cup of tea?' asked Megan, getting out of the wheelchair.

'It's all right,' Gillian said, rushing forward, looking slightly alarmed. 'I can . . .'

'You sit down,' Megan said. 'I'll do it. I could do with a stretch. Come into hospital and immediately they try to make you stay in one place . . . Wheelchair's the sympathy vote.'

She found a clean mug and filled the kettle.

'I shouldn't have come,' said Gillian in a low voice.

'Oh, he's always busy. He won't be long.'

'No, I mean . . .'

Megan waited, but whatever the girl meant, she was unable to say it. 'He must be a hard man to track down . . . what with working at night and all.'

'Yeah, he is.'

'You know, I have the same trouble with my Ted, and he works the same hours I do!'

'Look, I think I'm going to go,' said Gillian. 'Tell him I'll ring him.'

'Now, give him a few minutes,' Megan urged. 'At least have a cup of tea.'

'I don't want a cup of tea. I – I don't know why I came, really. There's nothing I have to say to him, nothing that can't be said over the phone. I'll ring him later.'

'Are you sure that's best?' Megan paused, then decided. 'I know it's none of my business, but after what happened the other night, and you being here now . . . well, he might feel very strange if you just leave without seeing him again.'

'He wouldn't give a toss,' said Gillian. Her voice was bitter, but the pain on her pale face twisted Megan's heart.

'That's not so,' said Megan gently. 'It would hurt him. He cares what happens to you, you know . . . he cares about you very much.'

'If he cares, he's got a bloody odd way of showing it. I mean, he can't even touch me without having to pat me like a dog. It's been nearly two weeks since I've been back. He hasn't even bothered to ring me. I don't know what he thinks he's waiting for. It's the same with Mum. When she left him. He just does nothing. Stands there soaking it all up. And everyone says, "Poor Ewart . . . he's so overworked . . . he's so patient". Look at you, making excuses for him. Just you try living with it. Sent Mum round the twist. That's why I had to get out. She was on ten milligrams of valium a day, last year.'

Gillian drew a long, shaky breath. Then she said, more quietly, as if passing sentence. 'That's not marriage. That's a farce. Sorry, I've got to go.'

This time, Megan did not try to stop her.

Alone again, she went back to her wheelchair and sat down, thinking about other people's problems.

She wasn't sure how much time had passed when Ewart returned.

'Sorry, got tied up with maintenance,' he said.

'She's gone,' said Megan, although he could see that for himself. She watched him, aware that he was uncomfortable.

He shifted awkwardly from one foot to the other. 'Did . . . did she say anything?'

'Something, yes.'

'She's a strange child.'

'She's not a child, Ewart,' Megan said, exasperated by his obtuseness. Since Gillian wasn't here to speak for herself, Megan would have to do it for her.

'No, no, no, of course. I only meant . . . you know what I mean.' He looked at her pleadingly.

Megan just managed to stop herself from nodding or saying something understanding. Gillian's voice still rang in her ears: 'Look at you, making excuses for him. Just you try living with it.'

'I think maybe it'd be a good idea if you gave her a ring. I think she'd appreciate that,' Megan said.

'I've been meaning to.' Ewart sank into the chair nearest Megan.

'I've just been dealing with a mother who's lost her child. Alcohol and amyl nitrate. Nothing anyone could do. She thinks we could have saved him, thinks we did something wrong . . . she says he was a good boy, never drank, it couldn't have been his fault, so it must have been ours. Nothing we say can be right. Total misunderstanding, on all sides. Crossed wires everywhere.' He looked down at the floor. 'Do you think everyone goes through a time when they think "Where's it all gone wrong . . .?" Sounds corny, I know.'

'No, it doesn't. It sounds like life.'

He smiled, grateful for her understanding. 'I'm having to argue with some particularly stupid bureaucrats at the moment – every day, it seems like. And it's always the same thing. Closure. I sit there, on the phone or in the meeting, and I suddenly think, "What in heaven's name am I doing here?" But I stay, of course. I have to, have to try, have to keep on fighting, for the rest of you lot, and for the people who need us, for what we stand for . . .' He looked at her, eyes pleading for compassion. 'I mean, if Gillian knew what I was going through, if she could try to understand that for a bit . . .'

Megan felt pulled in two directions. She knew, as well as anyone, how important this issue was, and how much they needed Ewart to go on fighting for them. On the other hand, she knew what Ewart's otherwise praiseworthy devotion to duty had done to his marriage, and, even more tragically, what it was doing to his only daughter. Ros Plimmer had chosen her husband, with all his flaws and weaknesses as well as his strengths. Nobody had forced her to marry him. It took two people to make or break a marriage. But Gillian was the innocent victim of her father's obsession.

'Ewart,' said Megan. 'You're her dad, not her employer. Right?'

He didn't reply at first. He looked at the floor. Then he stood up.

'You should be in bed,' he said gently. 'I'll find Charlie, and get him to take you back.'

When he had left the room, Megan realized just how tired she was. She also felt sad; sorry that she hadn't managed to come through for Gillian.

But how could she? Ewart had had a lifetime's practice at avoiding emotional responsibility. His work was his life. Where Megan tended to react to people, even strangers, as if they were family, in need of mothering, Ewart's approach was the complete opposite. To him, personal ties were trivial. What mattered was the public, and his work. If Gillian wanted his attention, she would probably have to become a nurse. Or, yet again, another sad victim rushed in to Casualty in the dead of night.

Megan prayed that Gillian would, from somewhere, find the strength to avoid taking that route.

# Chapter Ten

A nurse was beaming down at her, very close. As Megan's vision began to clear and things came back into focus she saw first the nurse's friendly face and then recognized the bundle in her arms for what it was.

'Here you are, m'dear,' said the nurse in a broad West Country accent. 'You've had a lovely daughter. Can you sit up? Would you like to hold her?'

There was nothing in the world Megan wanted more than to hold her new baby, but sitting up was quite beyond her. She didn't think she'd ever felt so tired in all her life. It was as if she was completely without bone or muscle.

But at last she managed to put her arms out, and the nurse settled the warm, living bundle into them, close to Megan's breast.

'There now,' said the nurse. 'Isn't she a beauty?'

And she was, oh, she was. She quite took Megan's breath away, she was so beautiful. Tiny, and brick-red in colour, with a little fuzz of downy black hair covering her fragile skull. Perfect tiny ears, perfect tiny fingers fidgeting as she slept, a rose-bud mouth and soft, smooth nubbin of a nose.

While Megan gazed adoringly at her, amazed that this perfect, living creature could have come from her own body, the baby opened her eyes. They were large and deeply blue, and they fixed upon Megan with an attention quite unlike the usually bland, unfocused gaze of the newborn.

The baby recognized her – Megan was certain of it.

And as she gazed into those blue eyes, Megan also became convinced that she knew the baby, just as it knew her. This was not their first meeting. Their eyes had met at some time in the past.

Then she had it.

Her baby's eyes, too wise and loving to be those of a newborn, were her mother's eyes. Her mother had come back to her, reborn as the daughter she had always wanted.

'Caithleen,' Megan murmured. 'I shall call you Caithleen.'

There were tears in her eyes, blurring her vision. She struggled to blink them away, desperate to keep Caithleen in view.

'Megan,' said a voice. 'Megan, can you hear me?'

It wasn't the Devonshire cream voice of the nurse – this voice was a London accent, and Megan recognized it as the voice of someone she knew. Yet she tried to resist it, tried to hold on to her baby . . . tried to hold on to her dream.

Megan opened her eyes, feeling a tremendous

sense of loss. There was no baby; there never had been. She'd checked in with a cancer, not a pregnancy.

'Megan? It's Nan. Can you hear me? How are you feeling?'

Nan Atkinson stood looking down at her. An old friend from student days, Nan had returned to Holby – and to nursing – only last year, after the break-up of her marriage.

'Thought you were in maternity,' Megan said.

'I was. This is a temporary assignment. Shortages, you know. If you can't afford to hire more people, move the ones you've already got around to make them look like more. How are you feeling?'

'Groggy.'

'Any pain?'

Megan shook her head . In fact, she could hardly feel her body at all. She was floating. It wasn't an entirely pleasant sensation, but it certainly wasn't painful.

'I thought . . . I thought I'd had a baby,' Megan said. 'The only other time I'd been in hospital, you see . . .'

Nan pressed her hand. 'Everything's all right,' she said. 'I jut wanted to tell you that. The operation . . . they caught it in time. It hadn't spread. You're all right; you're going to be all right.'

Megan was drifting again, not quite certain what Nan was talking about. She tried to smile, because that seemed to be called for, but she couldn't keep her eyes open any longer.

'That's right, sleep,' said Nan. 'Sleep all you can . . . that's the best thing for you, now.'

Next time, the pain woke her.

Like some thug which had crept into her bed while she slept, the pain squeezed her viciously. It moved all through her body, casually cruel, her new master.

Tears ran down her face unchecked. She was as bewildered by her own feelings as a newborn. She had never known such agony, had never imagined that the pain she had been told about would be like *this*.

'Time for your tablets,' said a voice, some uncounted time later.

Megan looked up blankly, not understanding.

'Lift your head, now, that's right . . . swallow.' A nurse she didn't know put two chalky tablets in her mouth, and gave her water to swallow them down. 'There's a good girl.'

Megan stared after the young nurse, walking briskly away, and had the strange, disorientating sensation of being in the wrong place. She, Megan, was the nurse; she was the one who should be saying, 'There's a good girl.' How did she come to be lying here, incapacitated by pain, taking tablets, weak and docile as a child?

*

116

Those first few days in hospital were a strange, blurred haze of pain – shocking in its ferocity, in its utter power over her – followed by the floating, detached times when the tablets moved the pain away from her, times of sleeping dreams and waking dreams.

Despite all her experience as a nurse, knowing how hospitals worked, and how patients reacted, Megan was unprepared for her own utter helplessness. Knowing something by observation or by fact was not the same as feeling it herself. She had known the fact that hysterectomy was a serious operation. Now she knew what that meant. She had not been prepared for the power and extent of the pain – perhaps that was something that no one could ever be prepared for until it actually happened. Before, she had been determined not to become overly reliant on drugs, and had made up her mind to refuse painkillers. Now, as soon as the effects of one tablet wore off she could only pray and count the minutes until it was time for another. Absurd to worry about drug dependency when without drugs the pain would consume her.

She slept a lot. When she was awake she spent most of her time listening to the radio, and letting her mind drift. Certain songs triggered memories as rich and vivid as dreams, and she seemed to live the past over again.

She remembered meeting Ted.

Neil invited him to dinner one Sunday. No advance warning; as usual, it never occurred to him that there might not be enough food to go around. He expected his sister to cope with an extra mouth to feed as capably as she coped with whatever else life threw her way – and of course she did.

Megan hadn't fallen in love with Ted at first sight, but it hadn't taken very long. She had been intrigued by him, especially by the contrast between him and the other men she knew. Most of Neil's mates were Irish and, like himself, self-assured, bouncy, talkative. Some of them tried their charm on Neil's sister, but she wasn't having any. She could never take their elaborate flattery or flights of fancy seriously, and she knew how to deflate them with a few well chosen words. Then there were the doctors and the medical students at the hospital. Most of Megan's fellow nursing students cherished a crush on one of the men in white, but although Megan was aware of their appeal, she never lost her head. They were simply out of her league, she thought. They belonged to another world. They were not for her.

Ted was something different. His silence and shyness she interpreted as romantic moodiness. He seemed so self-contained, so self-sufficient. And then there was his wonderful foreignness – his solid, undisguisable Englishness. He wasn't classically handsome, but she liked his looks, especially his eyes, and there was an animal magnetism to him that alerted her whenever he came into the room.

He was attracted to her, too. She could tell by the way he watched her; he didn't have to say a word. And he didn't say a word. After a while, Megan began to wonder if he would *ever* declare his interest.

He came by the flat with Neil; he came to tea or dinner whenever invited; but he never made any attempt to see Megan on her own.

Gradually realizing that this solid, self-sufficient young man might actually be shy, Megan plotted to make things easier for him. One Sunday, a few minutes before Ted was expected to arrive, Megan sent Neil out to buy a newspaper. She told him to take his time about it. He was not to return for at least half an hour, and an hour would be even better. He needn't worry about missing his dinner – she'd timed it so it wouldn't be ready for an hour and a quarter. If Neil came back in an hour, he'd have his usual meal, and her thanks. If he came back too soon, though, he'd be having cold dinners – or none at all – for the next month.

Neil grinned – Megan could see that she would be in for teasing, no matter how fiercely she scowled at him – but he promised he'd stay away for an hour, and he did.

Encouraged by Megan's interest, and uninhibited by Neil's presence, Ted relaxed, and talked more in one hour than he had in three months previously. He even plucked up the courage, before Neil returned, to invite her out.

After that, things had moved more swiftly, as they got to know each other and fell in love.

Megan smiled to herself, eyes closed, as she remembered the first time he had kissed her. The first time they had quarrelled. Misunderstandings, followed by deeper understandings. The time he'd taken her to a really posh restaurant, for her birthday . . .

She was wrenched out of the past and deposited firmly back in the far less pleasant present by the arrival of Bernard and Tom, both looking distinctly uncomfortable in the alien hospital atmosphere.

Oddly, the hardest thing about the hospital stay for Megan – normally such an easily social person, always someone who hated idleness and had no particular love for being alone – was the visitors. It seemed that everyone she knew was determined to come and visit her. Her family, her friends, her neighbours, her workmates, all the people she saw regularly, and quite a few she didn't. It might have been gratifying, learning that she had so many friends, that she mattered to so many people, but the truth was, she would rather have been left alone until she felt better. She didn't like to be seen weak and helpless. It was such an effort to be 'good old Megan' for everyone as usual, and yet it was an effort she made and went on making. And she was successful. Everyone who came to visit was relieved and pleasantly surprised by how well Megan looked, and how cheerful she was. And the prognosis was good; the operation had been a success. They could stop worrying about her.

Ted came by ten minutes before the end of visiting hours. Dave and Anabel took his arrival as their cue to leave.

'Meet you outside, Dad,' said Dave as they went out.

Megan was nonplussed. She had been certain that Ted wouldn't come – she knew how he felt about hospitals, and she had told him not to bother visiting.

'I brought you some flowers,' he said awkwardly, revealing a bunch wrapped in cellophane.

Megan nodded, uncertain how to react. It was odd, too, after remembering the younger Ted so vividly, to see the middle-aged man he was now. Flowers had never been part of his repertoire . . . but taking flowers to someone in hospital was not really a romantic gesture.

'Did the boys put you up to this?' she demanded.

Ted looked hurt. 'No! What do you mean? I wanted to see you; I was worried about you.'

'Well, there's nothing to worry about – I told you that! If you didn't believe me you could have phoned the desk. You didn't have to come in yourself.'

'I thought you might be glad to see me. I can go

away again if you want.'

'Don't be daft.' Megan sighed. 'Sit down.'

He laid his bunch of flowers on the bedside table, beside the vase of tulips, and sat on the straight-backed chair that had been pulled up close to the bed.

Then they looked at each other in silence. Megan thought about explaining to him that she'd been talking to people all day, and that she wasn't really up to the demands of more conversation, but even such a statement seemed to require too much energy. So she said nothing. She just looked at him, and he looked at her, and somehow the very fact of his presence, so solid and familiar, was comforting in a way that all the concern and talk and advice and gifts from other friends and relatives had not been. Ted wasn't asking for anything, and his only gift was his presence. But that was enough. It had always been enough.

She sighed again and the tension went out of her body. Her eyes wanted to close, and so she let them, knowing that Ted wouldn't be offended.

After a moment she felt his fingertips against her face, brushing her hair back away from her eyes.

'Funny to see you like this,' he said softly. 'Usually I fall asleep first. You're always moving, always doing something. For as long as I can remember. No, don't move . . . stay like that. You rest. Go to sleep, love. It's all right. I'm here.'

*

Megan knew she was on the mend when she began feeling bored. Sleep became less important, and she was more grateful for visitors bringing her news of the real world. Outside of regular visiting hours, her friends from Casualty stopped by for a chat whenever they could spare a few minutes from their busy shift. Megan was grateful for that – she liked the sense of connection, liked the fact that she was still considered part of the team, even if she wasn't active at the moment. And she liked the way the younger nurses turned to her for advice – although she made a joke of enjoying playing the role of the 'wise old woman' who handed out the solutions to other people's problems, there was a hard core of truth at the centre of that joke.

'Ever think of becoming an Agony Aunt?' Susie asked once, having just spent the past half-hour perched on the edge of Megan's bed, telling her about her latest unsatisfactory boyfriend. 'You'd be terrific!'

'Nonsense,' said Megan, embarrassed as she always was by praise. 'I don't have any talent for that – it's all just common sense!'

'It may be common sense, but most people don't have it. You should have a go – I'll bet you'd be great at solving other people's problems.'

'Even if I wanted to, I couldn't solve other people's problems,'

'Sure you could! Look what you just told me –'

'I didn't tell you anything. I only asked you why you thought you wanted to go out with this bloke who you just described to me as having all the social graces of Attila the Hun, a sense of humour King Kong could be proud of, and an ego the size of a cross-Channel ferry.'

Susie giggled. 'I didn't say that!'

'No, but you recognize him from that description, don't you? Ah, Susie, love, I couldn't tell people what to do. At least, I hope I wouldn't. I just believe in a few home truths . . . especially when it looks like people are lying to themselves. Sometimes your friends can point out the very things you'd like to overlook. If I can do that for my friends, I'm happy. But I can only do it for my friends, and only if they ask me. I couldn't meddle in the lives of strangers.'

'It's not meddling,' said Susie. 'And I'm grateful.' She jumped up. 'Now I've got to go – anyone else can piss off to the staffroom for a cup of tea whenever they like, but if I'm not behind my desk from exactly seven p.m. to seven a.m. there's hell to pay.' She dropped a kiss on Megan's forehead and was off.

Kuba followed soon after. Kuba was Megan's most constant, energetic and devoted visitor, bringing her news, gossip, long, rambling episodes of the epic misadventure which was his life, and flowers stolen from other wards. She was usually glad to see him – he made a change from the boredom of the long hours spent recuperating in a hospital bed – but too often all Kuba offered was another kind of boredom. It never occurred to him that he might have outstayed his welcome, and because she knew he meant well, Megan found it difficult to tell him when she wanted him to leave. As a result, she sometimes took the coward's way out, pretending to have fallen asleep, and waited to hear him tiptoe heavily away before daring to open her eyes.

Tom, Bernard and Dave had made their regulation appearances as dutiful sons on the first day. After that, readily convinced by Megan's assurance that she was fine and wanted for nothing, they did not return. She missed them, but she was too proud to ask them to come back. Even if she did, she thought, they would be coming under duress, and she didn't want that. They were as uncomfortable in the surroundings of a hospital as their father.

Megan wondered sometimes what it would have been like to have had a daughter. She had hoped for a girl, before both Bernard and Tom were born, but she had not been dissatisfied each time by another son. After so many years of being the only woman in an otherwise all-male household, Megan could hardly imagine life any differently. It had all worked out for the best, she thought. It was only because she had so much time to herself these days, so much time for thinking, and dreaming, that a question answered long ago should resurface to tease her and make her wonder, 'What if . . .?'

To Megan's surprise, her eldest son's girlfriend, Anabel, became a regular visitor. Even more to her surprise, Megan found herself looking forward to Anabel's arrival every day. If her visits had started out of politeness or a sense of duty, this had not remained the case for long. She sensed that Anabel came back out of genuine interest and caring.

Megan liked the girl more and more. As she had sensed earlier, beneath the middle-class manners, posh voice and intellect a little too prominently displayed, Anabel had a good heart.

'Has David been in to see you?' she asked during one visit.

'No, love, but I don't expect him to.'

'He said –' Anabel suddenly shut up and tried to change the subject, but Megan sensed which way the wind was blowing.

'Don't,' she said to Anabel.

'Don't what?'

Megan couldn't help but smile at the mock-innocence. It was so like talking to a child of her own. 'You know what I'm talking about. Don't try to bully Dave –'

'As if I could!'

'Or wheedle or tease him or play on his guilt to get him to come see me. I could do that myself, if I wanted, and I don't. I miss my boys, but it doesn't do me any good to see them here under orders . . . heads down, tails tucked between their legs like one of the dogs dragged somewhere he doesn't want to go on a leash. I'm not dying –'

'Oh, Mrs Roach!'

'– so there's no need to drag them in to pay their last respects. This is no atmosphere for healthy young animals – I don't like it, and I've worked here, and places like here, half my life.'

'Your sons do miss you.'

'Yes, I'm sure. Miss my cooking. But it won't make them feel any better to come in here and see their mum lying flat in bed. Makes them nervous, I know that. They can't cope with seeing me an invalid. And why should they? I have what I need here, and I'll be home soon enough.'

Anabel looked down at her small, well-manicured hands. 'Would you rather be left alone? I mean would you rather I didn't come in?'

'Now, that's not what I mean at all! I enjoy your visits – as long as *you* do. It's seeing somebody who's nervous, somebody who'd rather be anywhere but here, that wears me out. I have to spend all my time soothing them, telling them that I'm fine, until it seems more like *they're* the one who needs special treatment, not me! Ted's dead scared of hospitals, you see, and I think the boys must have inherited some of that. But it doesn't seem to faze you, which means that I haven't got to spend all my time trying to calm you down, which means I can enjoy talking to you. Or listening. And besides, you bring the loveliest flowers.' Megan paused to gaze appreciatively at the bouquet beside her bed. 'I do love flowers.'

'So do I,' said Anabel. 'I always have bowls and vases full of them in the flat – I can never resist spending money on fresh flowers, even when it means I have to do without something else. I wish I could have a garden.'

'You know, when Ted and I were first married I used to have a window-box – that was all the garden I had. We could barely afford that, even though money seemed to go further in the old days. I used to go out to parks and public gardens and take cuttings for my window-box . . . Used to horrify Ted, who lectured me about my criminal tendencies.'

Megan began to laugh, and Anabel joined in.

Then Megan stopped with a gasp. 'Ooof, me stitches . . . they say laughter is the best medicine, but not . . . not when they've cut you open.'

Megan had gone pale, and was having a hard time keeping her voice steady.

Anabel leaned forward, alarmed. 'Mrs Roach, are you all right?'

'Fine, I'm fine. Just . . . shouldn't have laughed.'

'Do you want me to get a nurse?'

'I *am* a nurse, dearie.'

'I mean, do you need something?'

'Just . . . time,' said Megan. She closed her eyes, trying to get a grip on herself, on the pain that racked her. She wondered how long she would have to hold on before it was time for the next pain-killer, and was almost afraid to look at her watch, afraid the minutes would expand to infinity.

'I'll get someone, a nurse, she can give you something –'

'No,' said Megan. She knew too well, from experience on the other side, that patients were allotted only a certain number of pain-killers, to be given at certain times, and it was no good asking for more. The pain she felt was normal. It meant her body was healing.

She managed to look at her watch. Only ten minutes or so to get through, and then the nurse would come with the relief from this pain. She could bear it, knowing it had an end. She had to bear it.

Megan said to Anabel, 'Stay with me until the nurse comes. Talk to me, about anything. It won't be long.'

Anabel took her hand, and Megan squeezed it gratefully.

'Let's see,' said Anabel. 'Shall I tell you about . . . about the film Dave and I went to see last weekend? It was a pretty good one, but very strange. An American film called *Static*. It was about this bloke who invents a television that shows you what's happening in Heaven . . .'

# Chapter Eleven

Although she was still weak, and felt worse than she would willingly admit to anyone, Megan was finally allowed to go home.

'Hallelujah,' she said when Dr Baldwin visited her bedside with this welcome information. 'Someone else can have this bed – and welcome to it!'

'Now, Mrs Roach. Please remember that although I am letting you go home now, you are still an invalid. You are not fully healed, and you are not to behave as if you are. You must have plenty of rest – you must not over-exert yourself – you are to take as much time as you need to convalesce.'

'Now, Dr Baldwin,' she said, mocking him. 'You are talking to a nurse, you know.'

'That's precisely what worries me, Mrs Roach. If you weren't so accustomed to tending to the needs of others, you might have a little more respect for, and patience with, your *own* needs.'

'I'll look after myself. You don't need to worry about me.'

'But I do, Mrs Roach. I do worry about you.'

Fear stabbed through her at his words; her hands

clenched at her sides. 'What do you mean? I thought there wasn't any need to worry.'

'Not if you take proper care of yourself,' he said, and she relaxed, although still annoyed that he had frightened her.

'I'll be the perfect picture of a model invalid,' she said. 'Sure I will, Dr Baldwin.' She gave him a sunny smile.

He didn't look as if he believed her – and really she couldn't blame him.

It was obvious from the way Ted treated her that Dr Baldwin had had a word with him first, and probably read him the riot act about ensuring that his wife got plenty of rest and didn't have to work or worry.

And maybe it wasn't such a bad idea. The short journey between Holby City Hospital and her home left Megan feeling drained and tired. All she wanted was the comfort of her own bed – far more appealing than the hospital bed – and the chance to sleep.

For the first two weeks at home, Megan was, as she had promised Dr Baldwin, a model invalid. Friends fulfilled their promises of coming in to help out by doing the housework and cooking, and despite her anti-cooking bias, Anabel proved to be quite capable around the house, particularly when working in tandem with Dave.

Megan could hardly believe what an organized and efficient housekeeper her eldest son had turned out to be. He also chivvied his younger brothers into a form of tidiness which, although it was below her own standards, was far higher than she would have dreamed possible from any of the boys. Megan supervised, when necessary, from the sofa or her bed; she was kept amused by friends, family and the dogs; she listened to the radio, watched television, leafed through magazines and even did a little reading. After the blankness of hospital life, just being home was a rich and rewarding experience . . . and also tiring. Megan slept more than she had since she was a baby, and, slowly, surely, she began to heal. She didn't miss her work at the hospital as much as she had expected; but she knew this enforced holiday wouldn't last forever.

Her holiday ended much more suddenly than she had imagined, however. One day, long before she was well enough to go back to work, Megan was unexpectedly thrown back into the drama of the Casualty ward, in a way and for reasons no one could have foreseen.

It was a little past eight on a Thursday evening, and Megan was alone in the house, except for the dogs. Ted had gone to work, Dave was over at Anabel's, Bernard had gone off to his science fiction enthusiasts' meeting, and Tom was auditioning for a newly-formed thrash band – whatever that meant.

Megan's sleeping hours were erratic. She thought

she might as well continue to sleep during the days, when Ted did, but there wasn't much to do at night, if Ted was gone and the boys out or asleep, and she still needed far more sleep than she had when she was well, with the result that she tended to sleep a few hours here, a few hours there, all through the day and night.

She had been asleep for less than an hour when the knocking came at the door.

Megan didn't hear it. She'd put her earplugs in, the well-established habit of someone who must sleep when everyone else is awake, and the distant sound did not penetrate.

Nor did the sound of the doorbell, nor the police radio and the excited voices on the street outside.

Not until the dog, Oliver, decided that there was something peculiar going on and his mistress must be informed about it, did Megan begin to emerge from her sleep.

Bowson was probably hiding under the kitchen table, or in the downstairs loo – his usual refuges whenever life got too confusing for him, which was often. Oliver had a different temperament, however.

Megan never knew whether Oliver just didn't care for barking, or if he knew about her earplugs. He certainly acted as if he knew. After a few minutes during which he gravely observed the activity outside from two vantage points – the front room window downstairs, looking out on the street, and

Megan's bedroom window, overlooking the back garden – Oliver made up his mind.

He went to Megan's bed, inserted his nose beneath the duvet, and pushed Megan's arm.

Megan stirred without waking, pulling her arm closer to her body.

Oliver moved a little closer. He rested his head on the edge of the bed and gazed at Megan's sleeping face. Then he nuzzled her neck.

The touch of his cold, wet nose on her tender flesh made her flinch, and she woke up all the way.

'Oliver!' she said, surprised, when her eyes opened.

He wagged his tail, and whined low in his throat, expressing urgency in the way he shifted on his legs.

Megan took her earplugs out. 'What is it, boy?'

Even as she spoke, she could hear an unusual level of noise from outside.

'What's going on?' she wondered. She got out of bed and went to look out the front window.

She saw three police cars outside, one just arriving. As she watched, policemen were moving quickly and purposefully along the street, and the road was being cordoned off.

'Well, whatever in the world . . . ?' She looked down at Oliver, shifting edgily at her side, and patted him firmly on the head. 'Good dog,' she said. 'Good dog!'

Then she was quiet for a moment, listening to the commotion outside and gazing out the front window as she tried to make sense of what she was seeing. Was it a drugs raid? Or terrorists? There were some strange-looking types a few streets over, but this street was very solid and respectable. Megan knew everyone who lived here – she had known them for years, and she would as soon believe one of her sons involved in drug dealing as any of her immediate neighbours. There must be some mistake, she thought, a false tip-off, a wrong address, some unfunny prank.

She heard voices from the back of the house now, and crossed the room to have a look out the other window. As she gazed out across her garden, at the backs and sides of neighbouring houses, she saw that there was a policeman crouching behind her garden wall. There were police in all the nearby houses and gardens, and some of them, she saw, were armed. And they all seemed to be focusing their attention – but cautiously, as if it might be dangerous to go too close – on old John Collee's house.

The Roaches had known the Collees for years, although for most of that time they had been friendly neighbours, rather than actually friends. There had been a time when Bernard was sweet on the Collee girl, Shirley, but she was several years older than he was, and didn't especially appreciate his devotion. Four years ago Miriam Collee had left her husband. Megan didn't know if Miriam had actually run off with her hairdresser, as local gossip would have it; she suspected some reason both more complicated and more mundane for the collapse of the Collees' marriage. Certainly Megan had been aware, along with everyone else who ever set foot in the Collee house, that there was a powerful and unpleasant tension between husband and wife for a good two or three years before she finally left him.

Miriam probably had good reason to leave her husband. He was not an easy man to get along with, and was something of a loner. Yet Megan's sympathies were with her husband. He was a sick man when she left him, and had been in and out of hospital for years.

Megan had not seen Miriam Collee since she left her husband and left Holby. Shirley made occasional, dutiful visits, and presumably kept her parents informed about each other.

After Miriam left him, John Collee had become one of the neighbours Megan kept an eye out for. Because she found it hard to believe that a man on his own would look after himself and eat sensibly, Megan was always dropping by with 'extra' pies or soups, claiming she'd made too much for her family to eat and insisting that he take it.

His house was always clean enough – if faintly musty-smelling from the stacks of newspapers and magazines he always had around – and Megan had to admit that he seemed to manage perfectly well without a housekeeper. He had been out of work for several years – it might have been early retirement, or redundancy, or for reasons of health. Megan didn't know, because he never volunteered the information.

And she probably wouldn't have known that he was eaten up with cancer, dying slowly despite all the specialists could do for him, if she didn't work in the hospital herself. He wasn't a complainer, John Collee. He didn't tell his neighbours about his troubles, but kept them to himself.

She hadn't seen him lately, Megan realized, as she stood staring across at his house from her bedroom window. She had been so preoccupied with her own illness . . . she hadn't seen or spoken to him for months, maybe for as long as half a year.

What had been going on in that time? Could he have moved? Taken in tenants? No, if either of those things had happened, Megan would have heard from one of the other neighbours. She tried to remember what gossip Sarah had told her; had she mentioned anything about John Collee, anything at all? Megan didn't think so. Once the gossip about Miriam Collee had died down, no one had given much thought to John, a man who tended to keep to himself.

'So what the hell is going on?' muttered Megan. 'Hey, Oliver?'

Oliver wagged his tail.

Outside, police were moving with professional swiftness and caution. Whatever it was, it was something big – no suspected burglary, no mere matter of unpaid parking fines.

Armed with revolvers, police were moving to isolate the shed that stood between Megan's garden and Collee's. And, unless Megan's eyes were playing her up, she saw someone who might have been a police sniper settling into position at an open, upstairs window in one of the houses opposite.

It was like watching television, Megan thought. She could scarcely believe it was all real, all of it taking place in the familiar surroundings of her own home.

And where, she wondered, was everyone else?

She heard voices, distorted over police radio: 'One-four-three to Foxtrot. We're in position.'

'Foxtrot to One-four-three. Understood.'

'Foxtrot,' Megan said. 'Bloody silly army games . . . police training. They all watch too much television, hey Ollie?'

Oliver licked her hand.

'Thank you,' said Megan. 'That's convinced me I'm not dreaming – better than pinching myself.'

There came the sound of someone blowing into a megaphone, and then the loud, unnaturally projected voice: 'Can you hear me, John? I'm Andrew. I'm the negotiator. Just shout if you can hear me. Then we can talk.'

There came a rather wavering shout – it seemed to be a 'Yes'. Megan couldn't recognize the voice from that one word. It might have been John Collee – she had noticed the negotiator was speaking to 'John' – but it might just as well have been anyone else in John Collee's house.

It had to be someone else, she thought. It had to be. John Collee was no criminal. She stroked Oliver's floppy, silky ears, seeking some sort of comfort from the touch, and continued to stare in concerned puzzlement out her bedroom window.

There was the negotiator – Andrew, he said his name was – holding the megaphone. A couple of policemen, one young and nervous-looking, covered him with their guns. Megan wondered what they thought they were protecting him from.

After a brief, incomprehensible conversation into his personal radio, the negotiator again switched on his megaphone and broadcast his voice into the still, early evening air.

'Right, then. OK John. We're listening. Just tell me what you need and I'll see what I can arrange.'

Staring out, baffled, Megan caught sight of a figure through the window of the garden shed. She strained forward, trying to see more, but whoever was in there was not taking any chances. He wasn't going to frame himself in the window for the benefit of a police sniper.

He moved forward and then back, and, along with

the police, Megan heard, 'I want press, radio and TV and I want them now!'

The negotiator shifted uneasily. 'Well, now, John, well . . . I need to talk to my boss. I'll see if I can fix something up.'

'Do it!' came the response. 'Do it now . . . And get a move on, or I'll shoot the child!'

Child? What child? Megan felt a chill at the words. Was there a child in danger? Being held hostage by some madman with a gun? That certainly seemed to be the implication, and yet she couldn't believe it. Now that she had heard more she felt convinced that the man in the shed was John Collee – the neighbour she had known for years.

'John, I can't arrange press without talking to my boss. Just give me a few minutes to sort something out, OK? I'll see what I can do.'

Megan couldn't wait any longer. She had to know; she had to try to help if she could. Not even pausing to grab a dressing-gown, going as she was, in her pyjamas, Megan hurried out of the bedroom and down the stairs to the kitchen, and then out the kitchen door into the back garden.

'What the hell is going on down here? What the hell is going on?' she demanded.

The young policeman who had been crouching beside the garden wall dashed towards Megan, coming in low and fast. He grabbed her around the waist and pulled her to the ground.

'Get down!'

Megan had no time to decide how to respond; the man half pushed, half pulled her down with him.

Speaking urgently into her ear the policeman said, 'This is no place for civilians! You shouldn't be here –'

'I live here!' said Megan indignantly.

'You should have been evacuated! There's a hostage in your neighbour's shed – a man with a gun, holding a child hostage!'

'But why? That doesn't make sense. John Collee wouldn't – that's John Collee, I've known him for years.'

Megan tried to sit up, but the policeman kept her down. She managed to lift her head, and looking towards the shed she could now see, quite clearly, that she had not been mistaken. It was John Collee who was in there. He was standing in the doorway, clutching a tatty old box-file in one hand, and a rifle in the other.

'I haven't got all night,' said Collee desperately. 'I want the television and radio and I want to speak to them now – I want to speak to the public, do you hear me? I haven't much time – please!'

With a kind of eerie calm, all the more striking by contrast with Collee's agitation, the negotiator said into the megaphone, 'Just bear with me, John. I'm seeing what I can do.'

'I do not believe this,' said Megan. 'I see it, I hear

141

it, but I do not believe it. Please let me up, would you? Let me speak to him. I know him – he'll listen to me.'

The young policeman picked up his radio and spoke into it while Megan waited. 'Willett to Foxtrot. I've got a neighbour of Mr Collee's with me. Do I have permission to let her speak to him?'

'A friend,' said Megan firmly. 'More than a neighbour – a friend. Say that.'

He shrugged. 'She thinks he'll listen to her. Says she's a friend.'

'Go ahead,' said Foxtrot. 'Can't do any harm.'

'It better not,' muttered Willett. He gave Megan a look that said he thought she was no more to be trusted than her crazy neighbour, and then stood up, and helped her to her feet.

They walked across the lawn to the negotiator, who nodded at Megan. 'Right,' he said. 'Keep it brief, and speak slowly and clearly.' He handed her the megaphone.

Megan hefted its weight as she took it. Suddenly, her heart was pounding hard and she was aware of the onset of the debilitating weakness which always overtook her these days after too much exertion. Grimly, she ignored it.

'OK,' said Megan. She drew back, startled by the way her voice was amplified. She started again. 'Hello, Mr Collee. Hello. This is Megan Roach here. Can you hear me?'

'Yes,' said the voice from the shed.

Megan smiled, and gripped the megaphone more firmly. 'The police have allowed me to talk to you because I know you, and because I explained to them you didn't mean to do anybody any harm. That's right, isn't it, Mr Collee? John? You know this isn't going to solve anything, John.'

Her voice was calm, but through her mind ran all the television news pictures she'd ever seen of terrorists and madmen holding hostages, driven by some chance word to kill.

The John Collee that she knew – that she had thought she knew – would never harm anyone, she was certain. And yet, here he was, making threats. There must be someone inside her neighbour whom she had never met, someone formed by pressures and events she knew nothing of. Somehow, she had to reach that man, touch his sympathy, return his common sense. The police had to treat him as a criminal. Only she could treat him as a caring friend, and have a chance to make him understand.

'John,' said Megan firmly but calmly, 'Put that gun down, now, and come out, will you.'

The door burst open, and John Collee came out. He was wavering on his feet, and Megan saw at once that he was on the verge of collapse. She threw down the megaphone and dashed towards him.

'Hold fire!' shouted the negotiator as Megan moved. He tried to stop her, but he wasn't quick enough.

John Collee slumped to the ground. 'Tell every-body,' he said. 'Warn them, tell everybody what's happening, get me the press!'

The whole area was a sudden hive of activity. Two armed police officers followed Megan, one of them with his gun trained on Mr Collee, although the man was clearly no threat to anyone anymore.

Megan crouched beside her neighbour, unbutton-ing his jacket. She was shocked by the sight of him – how old and desperately ill he looked – but she was as steady and efficient as if she was back in the casu-alty ward and he a patient who'd just been rushed in.

'Are you all right, John?' she asked. 'It's Megan – can you hear me? Are you all right?'

Behind them, a young police officer came out of the shed after a quick search, shouting, 'There's no child.'

'Where does it hurt, John,' Megan asked. 'Are you in a lot of pain?'

He managed a very faint nod.

'All right, then, all right,' said Megan soothingly. 'Don't you worry, I'm going to get you to hospital. Don't worry.' She glanced around for someone in charge, saying, 'He's going to need an ambulance. Right now.'

'No,' said Collee desperately, fighting against his pain and weakness. 'No . . . the press. Just get me the press. Just get me the press. I must tell them . . . must . . .'

'Relax now,' soothed Megan. She stroked his head, feeling the clamminess of his skin. 'Just relax and don't worry. Everything's going to be all right. We'll tell them. You've just got to relax. Think about your breathing. Don't try to talk. Take deep breaths. That's right. Good man.'

Collee's eyes closed, and he seemed to be responding to her voice or her touch, no longer struggling quite so hard, although he still clutched the tattered box-file as if it were indescribably precious.

Still stroking his head and making soothing noises, Megan glanced up. A boyish-looking police constable stood over them, gun pointed carefully to cover John Collee while avoiding Megan.

As if he could do any harm in this state, thought Megan. She caught the eye of the P.C. He looked embarrassed, but the gun never wavered.

The ambulance was quick to arrive. It was staffed not by Ponting and Mute as Megan had more than half expected, but by a couple of men Megan knew less well. There was Rowson, a Rastafarian, and his partner, Buttimore, a wild-haired, wild-eyed Irishman who looked like a mad bomber but who was reputed to be a true-blue Tory and devoted Monarchist. According to Charlie Fairhead, Buttimore was forever pinning up pictures of the Royal Family in the cab of the ambulance.

Charlie was a joker, though. Megan was not particularly surprised to find no royal pin-ups inside.

Megan went along with Collee, and no one questioned her right. Rowson gave her an odd look, however.

'Have they changed the uniforms, then?' he asked.

Megan looked down at her floral-print pyjamas. 'It's to make the patients feel at home,' she said. 'You like it?'

'Lovely,' he said. 'Dead stylish. In you go.'

'Don't worry now, Mr Collee,' Megan said, settling herself beside him. 'We're on our way to hospital.'

'The press . . .' he said, sounding terminally exhausted.

'Yes, yes, we'll see about that just as we get you well.'

'Too late,' he whispered. 'Too late for me.'

'Shhh, shhh, just you relax, now,' she said automatically, although in truth she thought he was right. She had seen the approach of death too often to be easily mistaken. It probably was too late for John Collee. If not tonight, the end would come soon.

She looked at the armed police constable who was accompanying them, the same one who had been covering Mr Collee since his collapse. He looked confused, and no wonder.

'What's your name?' Megan asked.

'Grant.'

The ambulance started with a lurch that made Collee cry out. Immediately, Megan's attention was all for him.

'I know it's bad, Mr Collee,' she said. 'But just hold on . . . it won't be long now.'

'Um, Mrs?' said P.C. Grant uncertainly.

'Roach,' said Megan.

'Mrs Roach, do you think you could get him to give up that thing he's holding?' He nodded at the tatty old box-file which Collee still clutched protectively.

'Why?'

'Well, it might have a weapon in it, or something . . .'

'A weapon!' Megan said scornfully. She looked at P.C. Grant challengingly. 'The only weapon he had was an old World War II rifle that probably hadn't been fired in forty years and probably wasn't even loaded, either.' She saw by the look on his face that she was right.

'I have to take precautions,' P.C. Grant said. 'We can't assume anything . . . he did phone up and claim to be holding a child hostage and claimed to be armed; we can't ignore things like that, you know. We can't take chances with lives.'

Megan felt a little ashamed of herself for intimidating the young officer. He was only doing his duty, and behaving quite sensibly, really. She realized she was blaming him for Mr Collee's condition, and that was clearly silly.

'You're right,' she said gently. 'I'll try.'

But as soon as she touched the box, Collee reacted

by jerking away from her, and beginning to shake .
'Uh uh, no!'

'Now, Mr Collee, it's only me, Megan. I'm just trying to make you more comfortable. Why not let me
hold that for you?'

'It's proof,' he said. 'The only proof I've got . . . to
show the world . . . world's got to know . . . got to tell
the press . . .'

Megan looked at Grant. 'It's no good,' she said. 'He
won't let it go. I don't even want to try – I don't want
him getting upset. Right now my only concern is to
get him to hospital in one piece. Don't worry about
it . . . you can see he's no threat to you, can't you?'

Grant nodded. 'Anyone can see that, the only person in danger is himself.'

'Megan?' Although Collee's voice was weak, she
could hear the note of anxiety, and she hurried to
reassure him.

'Yes, yes, I'm still here. I'm still here. It's OK.'

'Where are we? When's the rattling going to stop?'

'We're on our way to hospital. Won't be long now.
It won't be long.'

He groaned. 'Christ! It's agony.'

'I know, I know. Just hang on, Mr Collee. We'll be
seeing a doctor soon.'

He was silent as the ambulance lurched and rat-
tled through the streets of the city. Then he said,
tapping the box he clutched so tightly, 'You got to
read this.'

'All right, Mr Collee. I will.'

'You got to read it tonight, Megan. No time to lose. Read it tonight, so you'll understand, so I can explain.'

'I will,' she said again.

'World's got to know . . . got to tell them.' His voice was growing weaker.

'Now, just relax, Mr Collee, will you please? I'll do what I can for you – I'll read whatever you want – but you've got to do something for me. Take it easy, OK? Don't worry. Everything's going to be all right.'

Collee looked past her, up at the police officer, and said bitterly, 'Aren't you lot ever satisfied?'

Grant looked embarrassed, and moved away, sitting down out of Collee's line of vision.

Megan's pity shifted from the dying man to the officer, and she said, 'Come on. It's not his fault, Mr Collee. Don't blame him now. He's only doing what he has to. What did you expect? You did put on quite a show out there, you know.' She stroked his head. 'Nearly there. Just hang on. Good man. You're nearly there.'

# Chapter Twelve

Clive King was waiting in the ambulance bay when they arrived.

Megan was first out of the ambulance, keeping up a steady stream of meaningless, hopefully comforting talk to the man on the stretcher. 'Here we are. No need to worry. Got you here safely.'

'Megan! What the hell are you doing –'

Megan looked at King. 'I'm loving my neighbour as myself. You didn't think I'd come here voluntarily in my pyjamas just to see you lot, do you?'

Rowson and Buttimore emerged with Collee on the stretcher.

Puzzled, King looked from Megan to Collee and back again. 'So what's the catch, then?'

'This here is Mr Collee,' Megan said. 'Mr Collee, we're at the hospital now. Now, Mr Collee, this is Clive King, a very good friend of mine.' She looked at King. 'John Collee is a neighbour of mine. I've known him for years.'

'Ah,' said King.

'And this is Constable Grant. We had a little shoot-out together, didn't we? But everything is all right now.' She patted Collee's arm. 'We're going in now. You're OK.'

King stared after Megan in bewilderment. If this was a ploy of hers to come back to work before the doctor agreed, it was pretty far-fetched. He looked at P.C. Grant. 'Was she joking?'

Grant shook his head. He was looking after Megan with admiration. 'No, he had half my shop round his back garden. Pretty heavy . . . she talked him out, though.'

'What's it all about?'

'Lost his marbles,' P.C. Grant said, after consideration. 'Poor old sod.'

'Lost his marbles?' King shook his head. 'Lot of that around here, lot of lost marbles.' The two men followed the others inside.

King caught up to Megan as she was leading the two ambulancemen with Collee into a cubicle. 'We'll just get you comfortable, Mr Collee,' she said.

King caught her arm. 'Megan, you shouldn't be doing this.'

'I didn't have much choice,' she said. 'I fell into it . . . in my own back garden.'

'You've done enough. There's nothing more you can do for him. Now go home,' he said. 'Get Susie to phone for a taxi – get your Ted round here to take you home.'

'No, Clive. I'm in it now, I've got to stay. He'll talk to me. He hasn't got anyone else, you see. His wife left years ago.'

Susie looked in, consumed by curiosity. 'What are you doing here, Megan? You're fast losing sympathy votes.'

Megan shrugged. 'Just a heightened sense of responsibility. You know me. Where's Baz? I want Mr Collee admitted. He'll need a bed upstairs.'

Susie gave her a big, bright smile. 'They're full.'

'And you're smiling about it?'

'What do you expect – tears? I've run out of hankies.'

Megan sighed. 'Nothing changes. Could you get Baz anyway?'

'I'll call her,' Susie said, vanishing.

'And tell Faith to look up his notes. John Collee. Should be thick as a book,' Megan called after her.

Collee groaned, and Megan moved closer to him. 'It's all right now, Mr Collee. Doctor will be here soon.'

P.C. Grant cleared his throat. He was shifting from one foot to another, and when he caught Megan's eye he indicated the corridor with his head. They both stepped out of the cubicle.

'Maybe you'd like to sit in the waiting room,' said Megan.

'I can't leave him – he's in custody.'

Megan gave him a look. 'He's hardly going to get up and walk out, now, is he?'

Grant looked more awkward than ever. 'I know, but . . .'

Megan patted his arm. 'But. You're only doing your job. I understand.

'He looks really sick,' Grant said. 'Is he going to die?'

She hated questions like that. But Grant wasn't a relative, so she didn't have to try to comfort him. She decided she didn't have to say anything at all.

'I'll stay with him till doctor comes,' she said, and retreated behind the curtain.

She heard King say, 'That man had half your shop out?' in tones of utter disbelief.

'Yeah, you scared them, all right,' Megan said quietly, gazing down at John Collee. 'You did that. But what was it all *for*?'

Collee's eyes were closed. He was pale and sweating and seemed to have moved to some other realm, where pain was the only reality.

She decided to let him rest, to have whatever peace he could find.

She left P.C. Grant standing guard in the corridor. 'Watch out for the gremlins,' she said in a conspiratorial tone.

He looked puzzled. 'What?'

'The gremlins . . . a well-known problem in hospital wards today. They're always stealing things . . . maybe even your gun if they can get away with it. Maybe even Mr Collee, who certainly couldn't walk out of here on his own. Don't say I didn't warn you.'

She found Baz with King in the administration

153

area, going over Mr Collee's file. It was as thick as Megan had warned.

'You shouldn't be here,' King said.

Megan decided to ignore him. 'Baz,' she said. 'Can you take a look at him?'

'I can take a look . . . I don't think there's much else I can do. Except try to make him comfortable.' She tapped the file. 'Four ops. Chemotherapy, and enough specialists to fill a stadium. It's a miracle they didn't bury him months ago.'

'Looks like they've chopped most of him out already,' King said.

'What are we going to do?' asked Megan.

Baz looked at King, and then at Megan. '*We're* not,' she said pointedly. 'You're going home.'

Megan raised her chin. There was battle in her eyes. 'I promised Mr Collee I'd stay with him, and I will. If you won't let me nurse him, I'll stay as a friend. He needs a friend. He doesn't have anyone else. And he's very, very ill.'

'Megan. *You're* not well,' said King.

'I'm perfectly fine,' said Megan dismissively. 'Did you know the police want to arrest him?'

'We've heard about the great back-garden siege,' Baz said. 'And don't change the subject.'

'He's dying,' Megan said bluntly. 'I'm not. Anyway, it wasn't a real siege. The man can barely stand up, and he convinces the police he's armed and dangerous. I want to know why. So do the

154

police. Only difference is – he likes me more than he likes the police. So he may talk to me.'

Ewart Plimmer arrived at that moment.

Before he could comment on her presence, or her attire, Megan beat him to it. 'You look well, Ewart,' she said. 'Doesn't he look well, Baz?'

Ewart looked bemused. 'Sorry?'

'I need to borrow a cubicle,' Megan said. 'Just till you find him a bed. I'm sure you'll manage to find him a bed somewhere. But until you do, I'll be with him in his cubicle. You see, Ewart, the thing is, he needs to talk to someone he knows.'

'Megan, you shouldn't be here.'

'Maybe I shouldn't, but here I am, and here I'll stay. Maybe it wasn't by chance. I'm the only person here he knows. He can trust me; he may talk to me. I'm not arguing.'

'I'm a doctor,' Baz said. 'And I'm telling you –'

At that moment P.C. Grant came running up. 'He's – I think he needs someone.'

'I'll go,' said Megan.

'I learned a long time ago it's no good arguing with Megan when her mind's made up,' said Ewart.

'No way she should be out of bed,' said King. 'No way she can help that man.'

'You volunteering to carry her off and tie her down?' asked Baz.

'That lady should be in politics, ' said King, shaking his head. 'There's no stopping her.'

'Lucky for Mr Collee,' said Baz.

Mr Collee was in an alarming state when Megan and P.C. Grant arrived, thrashing around on his narrow trolley, and shouting. 'I want to tell the world . . . they must know . . . I'll tell them what happened to me!'

'Now, now Mr Collee,' said Megan as she entered. 'You take it easy . . . I'm here. You can tell me what it's all about. But you've got to stay calm. No sense shouting like that – you'll just wear yourself out.'

'You'll – you'll listen? You'll read it all and . . . tell everyone?'

'Yes,' said Megan firmly. 'I will.'

Megan heard Ewart say to Baz, as he moved away, 'I'm going to get that man a bed upstairs if it's the last thing I do in this place.'

'Now, don't you worry, Mr Collee,' Megan said, with renewed confidence. 'It's going to be all right.'

But of course it wasn't going to be all right. Despite the earlier sense of urgency about getting Mr Collee to hospital, there was very little that could be done for him now.

He'd had four operations so far, as well as courses of chemotherapy and other treatments, but there had come a point when surgery, radiation treatment and drugs were all ineffective. His illness was past curing, unless it was by a miracle, and the only thing that medical science could offer now was

shown we are unable, therefore, to recommend compensation for your current health problems." More waffle . . . it's signed Colonel Smallhurst.'

'The names don't matter with them – they're all the same, all part of the same cover-up,' Collee said.

Megan looked at the letter again. 'Military tests,' she said. 'What kind of tests would those be?'

'Bloody farce,' muttered Collee.

Megan leaned forward, compelling his attention. 'What were you testing?'

'Never told us,' said Collee. 'Never told us a bloody thing. I know now, of course.'

'What do you know?'

Collee closed his eyes. Sounding very tired, he said, 'They weren't no ordinary bombs.'

Bombs, though Megan. Cover-ups. She suddenly felt afraid. She glanced at P.C. Grant. He looked away. She chided herself for paranoia. After all, he was only a police constable, a local man. And far too young to have had any part in what Collee was talking about.

'Have you rung my wife?' John Collee asked.

'Yes,' Megan said. 'She's on her way, with your daughter. It may take some time.'

'Miles and miles,' said Collee. 'She didn't want to be around me anymore. Went right away. To Birmingham. She'd rather live in Birmingham than live with me, can you credit it?'

Megan smiled.

Collee noticed, and managed to twist his mouth in a sort of a smile in return. 'Yeah, lost my wife 'cause of all this. She said I was obsessed. Too bloody right I was! So would you be, so would anyone if you'd knocked your head against a brick wall.' He gestured at the file Megan still held. 'Never gave an inch. Fifty letters from the Ministry of Defence in there. Never gave a bloody inch!'

He was panting slightly, with exertion and pain. Megan wanted to help him, but knew there was nothing she could do. She had to let him talk. He had to tell someone before he died.

'There's other letters, too. I got to explain those. Let me show you –' He tried to sit up, but failed, fell back against the pillows, face contorted in agony.

'Take it easy,' said Megan. 'You don't have to go anywhere now. I've got the letters here – I'll find them. I'll read them to you and you can explain anything I don't understand.'

'You're not leaving?'

'I'm going nowhere.'

Duffy popped in a few minutes later, grinning all over her face. 'I've done it!' she said. 'A bed for Mr Collee in Lancaster Ward.'

'Isn't that Ortho?'

Duffy shrugged. 'Just for tonight . . . just till there's space in Medical. But I managed to get a bed! Pretty good, eh?'

'Brilliant,' said Megan. She was smiling, too. Duffy's pleasure was irresistible. Another small victory, she thought. But as she looked at John Collee, her smile faded. She wondered if he would be conscious long enough to appreciate his bed. She didn't believe he would survive the night.

'Get Kuba,' she said to Duffy. 'We'd better move him now . . . before somebody else steals that bed.'

As Kuba and Megan wheeled him towards Lancaster Ward, Mr Collee seemed to drift in and out of consciousness, forgetting what had been said to him, repeating himself.

'Did you get my wife?' he asked. 'You must phone my wife.'

'Yes, I told you, John,' Megan said. 'They've phoned your wife.'

'And they're coming?'

'Yes, she's coming. She's on her way.'

'With our daughter?'

'With your daughter,' said Megan, wearily. She ached. She was tired. She longed to lie down, but couldn't. She had made a promise to this man.

She looked at P.C. Grant, following along behind. 'Let's hope traffic is light tonight,' she said. 'Let's hope they get here soon.'

'Is he –'

Megan shook her head at him.

The night sister, an attractive young black woman Megan had not met before, met them when they reached the ward and led them to a small private room off the main ward.

'This is very nice,' said Megan, surprised. 'A bit of privacy . . . he needn't worry about keeping the other patients awake.'

Rather awkwardly, P.C. Grant gave Kuba and Megan a hand in transferring Collee from the trolley to the bed. If she had been in better health herself, Megan would have resented his interference. As it was, she had to be grateful for his help, since it meant she didn't have to lift the patient herself. When Mr Collee was in his new bed Megan fussed about rather unnecessarily, trying to make him comfortable, and trying to pretend she wasn't nearly too tired to move.

'Here we are,' said Kuba, beaming. 'Cosy like home, eh?'

'My last home,' said Collee. 'Home to rest.'

'Agh, don't be talking like that!' Megan admonished.

Collee simply looked at her, and she lacked the heart to go on, to peddle false cheer. He knew as well as they all did that he would die here.

'Can we go on?' he asked after a moment, quietly.

'Of course we can,' Megan said. 'I want to.' She pulled up a chair and sat down.

'I go now,' said Kuba, making a little bow.

Collee looked at him. 'Where do you come from?'

'I? Poland.'

'Poland,' said Collee thoughtfully. 'Do you have the atomic bomb in Poland?'

'The bomb?'

'Yes.'

Kuba smiled and shook his head. 'We have no bomb. But if we did, maybe it would be a different Poland. Maybe then my country would be strong.'

Collee closed his eyes. 'Strong? I don't think so . . . I don't know.'

'Oh, yes,' said Kuba. 'Strong. All the great strong countries have the bomb. Poland would be free. If only we had the bomb.'

He waited, beaming expectantly, but no one said anything. He nodded at the old man dying in the bed. 'Yes,' Kuba said. 'It makes you strong! Good night.'

'Maybe he's right,' said Collee wearily. 'Maybe that's the choice. Who am I to say what's best for Poland . . . or Britain? I never shirked my duty. If I have to die, to keep my country strong . . . but you'd think they might have told me. Told all of us. Given us a choice. Instead . . . instead of pretending nothing is happening. Even when it's obvious we're all dying.' He tapped the box file. 'Here, look in here . . . under "Personal".'

Megan dug out a wad of letters and began reading. She read quietly to herself for the most part, occasionally reading out a line or two to the dying man, to keep him informed of her progress, or to clear up some ambiguity.

These letters were both easier and more painful to read. Instead of the bureaucratic stone-walling of the official documents, these were personal, vivid slices of particular lives. They were letters from Collee's mates, the men he had served with in the mid-1950s.

In 1955, while Megan had still been a child living in Ireland, John Collee had been a young man doing his National Service. It was a part of life he had accepted without strong feelings. He had never considering enlisting, or of making the Army or the Navy his career, and unlike some of his schoolmates who felt, bitterly, that they had 'missed out' on the excitement by being born too late to fight in the war, young John didn't imagine there was anything romantic about battle. On the other hand, he didn't resent being asked to give his time and energy to serve his country. He didn't consider two years in the army to be an intolerable delay before he could get on with his 'real life' as some others did. On the contrary, he looked forward to a chance to get away from home.

'I thought I was going to see the world,' he said. 'Just like those old recruiting posters. And when I found out my tour of duty was going to be a tropical island, well . . . I thought I was a lucky sod. So did we all. We didn't know any better. They didn't tell us any different.'

Megan looked down at the sheaf of papers in her

hand, letters from a man called Jones, among others. Most of the letters were just ordinary, friendly letters about his daily life, his family, and his health. Occasionally they harked back to memories of the days when he had been serving with Collee, Blacker, Morris and others whose names he mentioned.

'But why do you want me to read this?' she asked. 'These are personal letters, from men I don't know anything about. What do they have to do with –'

'They have to do with what I'm dying of,' Collee said. 'They have to do with what happened to us all. They're proof. We all suffered. It's not coincidence – it's not chance, no matter what they said, those bastards at the MoD. Anyone who looks at these letters, who puts them together, can see. What's that one in your hands?'

'It's from your friend Jones.'

'What date?'

'Thirteenth of October . . . nineteen sixty-nine.'

Collee made a pained sound. It was obvious he remembered the letters, all the letters, very well. Megan wouldn't have been surprised to find he had them off by heart.

'Thirteenth October, nineteen sixty-nine,' said Collee. 'He wrote that two days before he died. He, was the first to go.'

'Of those of you who were on the island?'

Collee nodded.

'What happened to you there? What did you do?'

'Our job was to dig these huge holes in the sand and coral, put tanks and trucks in them. See . . . they wanted to know how they'd withstand the blast. Tanks and trucks. Never mind about flesh and blood. Never mind about us. 'Course, we didn't know then what kind of a bomb it was.'

'Didn't they tell you you might be in danger?' Megan asked, leaning towards him. 'Did you not suspect?'

'It was 1955!' said Collee. 'People didn't think about things like that then . . . well, not so much. We were kids, that's all. We'd just landed the cushiest Military Service you could dream of. Time of our lives, swimming, all these different kinds of fish, sunshine every day. Seemed like our worst problem was boredom. 'Cause if you got tired of swimming or fishing or sitting in the sun there wasn't much else to do. No discos, you know. There weren't any girls. We made a big thing out of mealtimes, invented new menus using all that fresh fruit and fish. I thought it was great. Thought I'd landed in paradise. Thought I might like to go back there when I was old. When I'd retired. Live out my last years in the sun.' His face tightened as the pain became almost too much for him to bear.

'Did we suspect anything? I don't know. Maybe sometimes I wondered why they were always scrubbing us down . . . they said it was hygiene and I thought, well, the tropics, can't be too careful . . . we were all a bit nervous about strange tropical dis-eases, exotic insects. Blokes told stories about spiders that would inject their eggs into your skin, or cen-tipedes that would crawl into your earhole while you were asleep. Horror stories about things like that. But not about the bomb. No, we weren't afraid of the bombs. You might not believe this, but we used to look forward to the explosions. Like I said, life could get a bit dull in a tropical paradise. So we enjoyed a bit of excitement. When the major said point your bum at the blast . . . should've heard what Blacker said!' He smiled.

P.C. Grant laughed.

Megan gave a start; she'd nearly forgotten the presence of the policeman. So, apparently, had Collee, who reacted to the sound from Grant with anger.

'Get him out – get him out of here. Now!'

Knowing it was a silly reason, Megan said, 'He can't leave . . . you're in custody.'

'I'm not running anywhere,' said Collee wearily. He closed his eyes.

Megan looked at the exhausted, emaciated, dying man for a moment. Then she got up and went to Grant who was standing more or less at attention by the door.

She smiled at him. 'Why don't you get yourself a cup of tea?'

Grant looked uneasy. 'Inspector might pop in.'

'I'll tell him you were caught short.'

Grant looked at Collee. It was clear the old man wasn't going anywhere under his own power.

Megan said in a reasonable tone, 'He wants to be alone for a minute, that's all. He's not about to beat me up and bash the door down, you know.'

She waited.

Then Grant nodded. 'Ten minutes.'

'Good man.'

When he had gone, Megan went back to sit beside Collee again. He still had his eyes closed.

'We alone?' he asked.

'Yes.'

Tears began to seep from under his closed lids, and he shuddered with sobs he could no longer repress. 'I'm so tired,' he said.

Megan held his hand. 'There,' she said. 'Of course you are. You have a right to be. But you don't want to rest yet, do you? You have something to tell me.'

'Thank you.'

'Now, don't bother with thanks. You want me to read these letters . . . all of them? I will. So I'll understand. And then what?'

'When I'm dead, there'll be only two of us left.' Collee looked at her. 'I know I shouldn't ask,'

'Go on.'

'Get a copy of these letters to Collins and Morris. Collins is in Australia. The addresses are in there.'

'Collins in Australia,' Megan repeated. 'Morris.

Copies of the letters to them.'

'Yes. I'm afraid . . . the Ministry of Defence'll try to cover up, of course. They may try to get hold of these, once I'm gone. Whatever you do, keep the originals.'

'What then? What do I do?'

'I shouldn't be asking you,' Collee said. 'It's not your fight . . . if there was anyone else who could carry on for me . . . Maybe Morris will do it. Maybe he'll be the one. He didn't want to know, before, but now . . . he can't pretend it didn't happen. He'll know he's in danger, too. Maybe he'll go to the press. If he doesn't, you'll have to. Someone must tell them, blow it open, let everybody know.'

'That was what you were trying to do with your siege,' said Megan. 'To get their attention. Well, you succeeded – it will be in the news. That'll have to get out – they can't cover it up. But . . . they may try to say it was for nothing. That you'd just gone crazy.'

'That's what they'd like to think,' said Collee. 'But if you think I'm crackers, just remember . . . I'm dying twenty years before my time.'

'I don't think you're crackers,' Megan said. 'I'll make sure they know.' But she felt sad as she spoke. Yes, she would do it. She would do as he asked. But she wondered what the point of it was. It was too late to save Collee, too late even to win the compensation from the Government that might have bought Collee a little more comfort in the last years of his life.

'Why did you never try the press before?' Megan asked. 'Why did you leave it so long?'

'You'll laugh,' said Collee. 'I wanted to beat them on my own. I don't want blood, I never did. Not revenge. Just . . . acknowledgement. They've got to admit responsibility. To admit they were wrong. And to make sure people know. So it can't happen again.'

Megan nodded, and reached out to press his shoulder.

'Police will try to get that off you,' Collee said. 'You hold on to it. Understand?'

'Yes,' said Megan.

'Don't let them cover it up, don't let them deny it. It's not just us who were affected, you know. I never knew how lucky I was, with my girl, that there's nothing wrong with her. Me mates weren't so lucky. Did you see the bit in Jonesey's letter, about his kid?'

Megan searched through the scrawled pages, eyes skimming over the lines, until she found it. She read it aloud, quietly. 'Sheila's just had another baby. She's a fantastic kid, but the doctor says her eyesight's a bit dodgy. I remembered Blacker saying his boy has something similar, so I thought I'd check with you 'cause I know you keep the file. Have any of the others had trouble with their children's health? I am a bit concerned that this is more than coincidence. Anyway, see you at the next reunion. Your old mucker, Jones.'

'Where is she?' asked Collee. His voice was thin

with pain. His eyes were closed. 'How much longer is she going to be?'

Megan stroked his brow. 'She'll be here soon.'

She was relieved when Collee finally dozed off, escaping from the ever-present pain. She could have slept herself, but remained sitting bolt upright, keeping herself awake by reading the letters that Collee had collected over the years in his file.

The door opened, and Baz came in.

'Megan?'

'He's sleeping,' Megan said.

'So should you be. You need your rest. You're still recovering, you know.'

'I'm staying till his wife and daughter come.'

'Take an hour in my room. Someone else can watch him.'

'No,' said Megan. Then, because she knew Baz meant well, she said, more gently, 'I'm sorry. I have to stay.'

Baz glanced at the sleeping man. 'Buzz me if he needs anything.'

'OK.'

'Be careful, Megan. Please.'

As Baz closed the door on her way out, Collee opened his eyes. 'Megan?'

'Yes, I'm here.'

'Nobody wants to take responsibility,' he said. His voice was very hoarse. 'All they ever said was that it was nothing to do with them. But men don't die like that, children aren't born like that by accident. The fact of the matter is the scientists didn't know what they were doing. They were messing about with something they didn't understand. Maybe they meant well. So did we. But we trusted them . . . and now they pretend not to know. I don't know whose fault it is. But I'm dying, and I'm bloody angry!'

He turned his head on the pillow. 'When did she say she was coming?'

'Soon. Soon. She said she would come right away . . . but it's a drive.'

'Please,' said Collee.

Megan reached out and took his hand. She was still holding it, trying to help him hold on to life, when he died.

# Chapter Thirteen

Megan faced a dilemma. Now that John Collee was dead, his possessions would pass, legally, into the hands of his relatives – presumably to his daughter, if not to his estranged wife. But because he had been in police custody when he died, because he had committed a crime, the police were sure to impound all of John Collee's belongings for a time at least, while they searched for the clue which would explain his behaviour and wrap up the case to their satisfaction. Megan would have been quite happy to leave the police, and Collee's family, to it. She didn't believe that the Holby constabulary could be connected with a Ministry of Defence cover-up, and she trusted they would return all Collee's precious files to his family when they had concluded their investigation. John Collee might believe that everyone was against him; Megan did not.

Anyway, it was police business, and she had no right to meddle. Although she had few qualms about taking from those who had to provide for those who had not when it came to practicalities on the ward, basically Megan was a good, law-abiding citizen.

But she was going to do what John Collee wanted, even knowing it was illegal. Because more deeply ingrained in her than respect for the law was a response to individual, personal needs. She honoured her promises, and she had made a promise to John Collee, not to the men who arrested him.

Maybe John Collee was wrong. Maybe he was paranoid. Maybe no one cared at all about his precious file of evidence.

But Megan knew she couldn't make that judgement herself. She had agreed to help him – and so she would.

She had decided upon a plan of action by the time he died.

When Baz answered her summons, Megan took the opportunity to slip away.

'I'm going to have a bit of a rest,' she said to Baz. 'If anyone needs me – '

Baz shook her head. 'You won't be needed – you might as well go home. It's all over, now.'

Megan looked at the dead man. It was over for him, she thought, but for some people it was just beginning. 'I meant the police might want to see me again before I go.'

'Oh, well, 'Baz shrugged at the incomprehensible ways of the police. 'I could probably deal with them, and his family, when they show up, but if you think –'

But Megan was already out of the door before Baz

had finished, before there could be any suggestion that she talk to the police *now*. Her heart was thudding painfully hard, but the rush of adrenalin through her system had flushed away all her pain and weariness. She was still clutching Mr Collee's box file, and no one had noticed.

She went as fast as she could go to the porter's lodge.

Fortunately, Kuba was in, feet up, watching an old-fashioned Western on the video and sipping a cup of his powerful Polish coffee.

'Kuba, I need you,' she said.

He leaped up. His eyes were gleaming, and he looked delighted. 'Megan, I am your servant!'

'Good. Because it is something quite tricky, and you mustn't tell anyone – no one must know you've done this.'

'Ah, Megan, you know you can always trust me! Anything you want, anything, ask me and I get it! What you need? Light-bulbs? Towels? Drugs?'

'Kuba, you are an angel – don't let anyone ever tell you different. No, it's nothing like that. Would you happen to know if there is a photocopying machine anywhere about the place?'

He nodded. 'Yes, I know where there is one. It is locked, the office, still, but I know where there is the key. Yes, I know.' He nodded thoughtfully to himself. 'But, I must tell you, Megan, I will do this, for you, but in only . . .' he paused to look at the clock on the video. 'In only two and one-half hours they will be unlocking the office and I think they will be noticing that it is gone, and then there will be trouble.'

Megan almost laughed. 'Oh, Kuba, I don't want you to steal if for me!'

'Is no problem! Is not very big! I put it on trolley, cover it with sheet and here we are!'

'No, no, it's very kind of you to offer, but all I want is to copy some papers, as quickly as possible, and without anyone else knowing. Could you take me to it? Do you know how to use it?'

'Yes, yes of course! Come with me – I take you now.'

Megan couldn't decide whether she felt more like a spy, or like an old fool reverting to her second childhood as she went sneaking, with Kuba, through the dark, quiet, largely deserted corridors of the big hospital.

She was glad that Kuba didn't ask her any questions. He simply accepted her need to do this, and helped her, as a friend.

There was a desktop photocopier in some administrator's office, with simple instructions for use taped to the cover. While Megan took a copy of everything in the file, Kuba stood guard. She was through in about fifteen minutes.

'Thank you, Kuba,' Megan said. 'I won't forget this.'

He put his hand over his heart. 'Megan, for you I

would do anything. It touches me so deeply that you are trusting me for this. I do not ask you why! In Poland, you know, these duplicating machines are forbidden.'

'Are they really?'

'Oh, yes. For if people can make many copies of things, they do not need to go to the newspapers or the official publishing houses which are controlled by the State. They can publish the truth, themselves, and everyone will read it and know the truth. You know it says in the Bible that the truth shall make you free? So, in Poland, and in Soviet Union, these copying machines are dangerous weapons, and they are forbidden to the people.'

'I need a box or something to hold these papers.'

Kuba looked around the office, and spotted a large, padded envelope, addressed to the hospital but empty now, and presented it, with a flourish, to Megan.

Megan put the original documents into the big envelope, and the duplicates into the box file. They wouldn't fool anyone who was looking for the originals, but Megan thought they would satisfy the police . . . particularly if the police weren't involved, and had no reason to suspect a cover-up.

'I have one more favour to ask,' she said.

'Yes, anything!'

Megan handed the envelope to Kuba. 'Will you keep this for me? Until I ask for it back. Better not let anyone know you have it. If it should come out, just say I left it with you and didn't tell you what it was.'

'I will not tell. You can trust me, Megan. I will keep them safe for you.'

'Thank you. I think we'd better go back now.'

Kuba reached out and put a hand on her shoulder. 'You look tired, Megan. You should take care of yourself.'

'Ach, I'm fine. Don't worry about me,' she said. She had to force a smile. 'You go on ahead of me, I'll take it a little more slowly.' Megan wondered if she was being silly, playing these secret service games. But she might as well do it properly. No sense hiding the documents with Kuba if she was going to walk arm-in-arm with him for all to see.

When Kuba left, Megan's energy seemed to go with him. It was as if she had been able to make an effort only as long as she had an audience. As she walked very slowly back to Casualty Megan realized that she was at the end of her strength. She couldn't keep going much longer.

One foot in front of the other, she told herself. One step at a time.

The police were waiting for her.

It wasn't only P.C. Grant – his superior, Inspector Kettle, was with him.

'Ah, Mrs Roach,' he said. 'Would you mind coming with us?'

'She's going straight home,' said Baz. 'She's not

well – can't you see? She's nearly dropping on her feet. She shouldn't have been here tonight at all. I'm sure your questions can wait till the morning.'

To Megan's surprise, Baz put a steadying arm around her. 'I sent for a cab,' she said. 'It's waiting for you in the ambulance bay now.'

'I'm all right,' said Megan. Even to herself her words lacked conviction. 'I can stay, if they want to talk to me – ' She looked at P.C. Grant as she spoke, and was amazed, even a little alarmed, by the way he was moving, one moment looming over her, and the next shrinking to almost nothing. She blinked, and realized that it wasn't Grant who was moving, but the room itself. The floor was pulsating and the air vibrating so that it was a wonder anyone could stand upright, she thought. Her knees buckled, and she swayed, and she would have fallen had not Baz been there to catch her.

Megan didn't talk to the police that morning. Two more days passed before the doctor allowed that Megan had recovered sufficiently from the effects of her 'dangerously foolish behaviour' to be allowed visitors.

She had been taken home in an ambulance after her collapse, Baz having ruled that any more time spent in Holby hospital, even if they weren't short of beds, was likely to be dangerous to Megan's health.

Baz also seemed to have appointed herself

Megan's personal physician, coming out to see her every day. Megan grumbled, but really she was grateful.

'It's like being under house arrest,' Megan said, propped up comfortably in bed.

'Too right,' said Baz. 'You should be grateful. Another break-out attempt and you'll find yourself back inside, under the eagle eye of Sister Newman.'

'Oh, spare me from Sister Newman!' said Megan, quailing in mock terror.

'It's up to you. No more running yourself ragged, looking after everyone except yourself. Next time you hear some excitement outside your window, leave it. Let the police take care of it.'

'And this used to be such a quiet neighbourhood,' Megan said. She shifted restlessly. 'Well, are you going to let the police come up now or not? I'm ready for the interrogation.'

'It had better not be an interrogation,' Baz said. 'They're under strict orders – no more than fifteen minutes with you. I can't stick around, unfortunately, so I've given your Tom instructions not to let them overstay their welcome. I think he quite fancies the idea of turfing out the coppers . . . you should have seen him grin.'

'Don't you go encouraging my innocent young son in his anti-social tendencies, Dr Samuels!'

'Me? I didn't have to – not with the mother he's got!' Baz grinned. 'I'll send the detective up.'

They didn't keep her long, and Megan suspected that orders from Baz had nothing to do with it. They'd already read through John Collee's file, interviewed others who knew him, and come to their own conclusions. The interview with Megan was a mere formality. She had nothing to tell them that they didn't already know, and nothing she said could move them in their belief that John Collee had been, as they put it, 'acting while the balance of his mind was disturbed.'

'He wasn't crazy,' Megan protested. 'You've read the file . . . you've seen the evidence he collected. The man died from cancer – eaten up by it! That didn't come from nowhere. He was exposed to massive doses of radiation in the 1950s. Are you going to sit there and tell me you think that's just coincidence?'

'I'm not talking about why he died,' Inspector Kettle said. 'That's not for me to say – that's for the experts to figure out. I don't really know how much radiation the human body can take without harm and, with all respect, Mrs Roach, I think even the experts aren't agreed on that. That isn't our problem. We're concerned with what he did before he died – it's his crime that concerns us.'

'It wasn't really a crime,' said Megan hopefully. 'No one was hurt.'

Kettle's expression chided her – without his having to say a word – for such wilful ignorance.

'It's a good thing no one was hurt – a very good thing. But even if Collee had no intention of hurting anyone, he knew he could make us believe he might. He cost the police a lot of time, energy and money, and for what? To draw attention to himself. That wasn't the act of a sane man.'

'It was the act of a desperate man,' said Megan. 'There is a difference. He was driven to it – time was running out for him, and he knew it.'

'And it drove him over the edge,' said Inspector Kettle. 'Quite so.'

'What's happened to his file?' Megan asked. 'All his papers?'

'They'll be returned to Miss Collee – his daughter. She being his nearest relation.'

Megan waited nervously for some suspicious remark or question about the contents of that file, but it did not come. Kettle asked her a few questions about what Collee had said to her before he died, and her opinion of his emotional and mental state, and then he departed.

It seemed he didn't suspect – that no one suspected. The papers were safe; Megan could carry out Collee's plans for them. Just the thought made her tired.

She reached for the telephone, and dialled Kuba's number.

'Kuba? This is Megan. Yes, of course I'm fine, just fine. Even Baz admits I'm allowed to have visitors now, so I wondered – yes, that's right; it would be lovely to see you. Oh, and Kuba – when you come, could you bring that envelope I gave you? Thank you.'

Megan put the phone down and sighed. She would rest easier once those papers were safely here, close to hand. It wasn't that she didn't trust Kuba, only things could go missing in a big hospital so easily. Maybe she didn't need to worry, but, as the saying went, even paranoids had enemies . . .

When Kuba arrived, he was bearing a bouquet, but no envelope. Had he forgotten it?

'Where's –'

'Shh!' Kuba put a finger to his lips and rolled his eyes expressively. Then he said, loudly, 'I have brought you these flowers, Megan. Where shall I put them?'

'There's an empty vase on the dressing-table, there, or you could ask one of the boys –'

'Yes, I will put them in the vase,' said Kuba. He put the flowers down on the dressing-table, and then unzipped his jacket. His expression cautioned her not to speak, so Megan watched, bemused, as he removed the envelope from its safe-keeping against his chest beneath the jacket. 'Yes, I have brought you these lovely flowers, lovely flowers,' said Kuba. As he spoke, he pointed at the envelope and mimed a question.

Did he think her bedroom was bugged, for the love of heaven?

It was hard to keep a straight face. However, Megan managed, and indicated that Kuba should slide the envelope beneath her bed.

This he did, with exaggerated caution. Then, straightening up, he said loudly, 'You look better, Megan. I am glad to see you looking better. I hope these flowers I have brought you will make you very happy. You must let me know if you want me to bring you any more flowers or anything else.'

'Thank you, Kuba, that's very kind of you, I'll let you know if I need anything.'

'Good,' he said. 'Very good. I go now, Megan, so you can rest and get better. I hope I see you soon. Goodbye.'

'Goodbye, Kuba. And thank you.'

'Is nothing! Nothing! Flowers . . . I can bring you flowers any time!' He nodded at the bed, raising his eyebrows knowingly, and departed.

He left just in time. She couldn't have held her laughter in a moment longer. She had to laugh – even though it hurt.

Megan frowned at the writing-pad on her lap and scratched through a line. Then she tore the sheet off, scrumpled it up, and dropped it to the floor to lie among all the other wadded sheets of paper, all the other false starts and abandoned drafts of the letter to Mr Morris. She wasn't very good at writing, and trying to write a letter to someone she had never met, to explain about John Collee's death and his last request of her, was particularly difficult. So the knock at her bedroom door just then came as a relief.

Gladly she put aside the writing-pad. 'Come in!'

A thin young woman with short brown hair and spectacles looked in. 'Mrs Roach?'

'That's right. Come in, dear.' Although Megan smiled a welcome, she was puzzled. She didn't recognize this visitor.

'I'm Shirley Collee.'

Megan gasped. 'Of course! I should have remembered.'

The young woman smiled tentatively. 'No reason why you should; it must have been ten years since you last saw me.'

'Sit down, dear, please. Would you like a cup of tea?'

'No thank you, really. I can't stay long – I have to catch a train. I wanted to see you before I left. I wanted to talk to you about my father.'

Megan nodded. She had been expecting this.

'You were with him when he died.'

'Yes. He kept asking about you and your mother . . . he did hope to see you before . . .'

'I wish I'd been there,' said Shirley. She cut off Megan's expression of sympathy with a hand gesture. 'I'd known for years that he was dying . . . I saw him when I could. Every time I came down to visit him I knew it might be for the last time. Still, even knowing that it was coming, I had hoped for more warning. I hoped for one more chance to see him; to say the things that, somehow, one never quite manages to say . . . '

'Some things don't have to be said. I'm sure he knew that you loved him.'

'He never told me!' Shirley burst out suddenly.

'What?'

'About the radiation; about the bomb tests; about why he was dying and his campaign, the way he was gathering up information from the men who had been on the island with him, and the letters he wrote to the Ministry of Defence, to the Government, to researchers, to anyone he thought might listen. I didn't know about that, about any of it!' She was silent for a moment, then, under control, went on.

'I only found out the truth after I read the file the police gave me. I'd left home before he knew he was ill. I was in Canada – I had a study grant when my mother left him. So I never really knew the reasons why; neither of them wanted to talk about it. I was told he had cancer – and I knew my mother felt guilty about leaving him when he was so ill – but . . . ' She shook her head, wonderingly. 'I can't believe it. The big cover-up. He was denying it to me, the same way everyone else was denying the truth to him.'

'Maybe he was afraid that you wouldn't believe him,' Megan said. 'Maybe he was afraid you'd respond like everyone else . . . and maybe he could take that from strangers, but not from his own daughter.'

Shirley nodded. 'Oh, I think I understand,' she said wearily. 'After all, he told my mother. She didn't want to believe him. So she left him. I think he was afraid I'd do the same thing. But I wouldn't have!' Her fists clenched in her lap. 'That's what's so frustrating – I would have believed him, I would have helped him. And now I can't. Now it's too late.'

'Your father didn't think it was too late,' Megan said. 'Too late for him, but . . . two of his mates from National Service days are still alive. A man called Morris, in Cardiff, and Collins, in Australia. He asked me to write to them.'

'You!'

'Because I happened to be there,' Megan said gently. 'I was there in your place. He left me his file.' She pushed the envelope across the bed to Shirley Collee, who stared at it.

'That's . . . the original?'

'Yes. He was afraid someone might get their hands on it and destroy it – he told me to keep the originals safe – so I made copies to give the police, and hid the original.' Megan made a rueful face. 'Not very law-abiding of me, I know.'

Shirley smiled. 'I was getting paranoid. I noticed they were all photocopies, but when I asked the police for the originals they denied all knowledge. I thought there was something fishy going on.' She touched the file. 'May I have this?'

'Of course. It's yours, as long as you mean to do something with it. If only for Morris and Collins' sakes.'

'Not only for their sakes,' Shirley said. 'It's a lot bigger than that, although I'm not sure my father realized. To me this isn't about getting compensation from the government for the lives of a few men who died because of what happened to them when they did their National Service; this is about the future. It's about making people aware of what radiation can do, *is* doing to all of us. We have to know, people have to speak out, and do research, and publish the evidence so that we can ask what *is* an acceptable risk? And who is it acceptable to?'

She leafed through the file, not really looking at the pages. 'Cancer is obvious . . . tumours . . . Everyone knows about that. People know about what happens when someone is exposed to a high dose of radiation; then it's obvious, cause and effect. But what about what it does to your children? What about genetic damage, mutation? That's so much harder to prove; mild mutations, genetic mistakes – these things can happen for other reasons; they happen in nature all the time.'

'Mr Collee – your father said that the children of some of the other men were affected –'

'So was I,' Shirley said. 'Although I can't prove it . . . if the MoD denied that my father had a valid

188

argument, they certainly wouldn't listen to mine.' She touched her glasses. 'Eyesight is inherited,' she said. 'My parents both have – had – almost perfect vision. Their parents never needed glasses, either. I have very weak eyes. I always have had. If I have children, they're likely to inherit my poor sight. I'm also asthmatic, and that's another hereditary condition. Only nobody can say who I inherited it from. You look sceptical.'

'No,' said Megan, although she was. Shirley's sincerity was evident, and Megan didn't feel she had the right to cast doubt on her belief.

'Why shouldn't you be?' Shirley asked. 'I was myself, for years. I can't prove I would have been any different, any healthier, if my father hadn't been exposed to all that radiation. Genetic change is part of life. There are natural mutations, genetic "mistakes" which don't have to be the result of an exposure to radiation. Only . . . it seems too much of a coincidence to me. And my mother's miscarriages. Oh, yes, she miscarried four times before she had me. It often happens. It might not have had anything to do with my father, only I don't believe that anymore. I've stopped believing in that kind of coincidence, just like my father did.'

Shirley Collee looked at her watch, and stood up. 'I have to go,' she said.

'If you'd like to come back again sometime, and talk more . . .'

Shirley smiled. It made her face much prettier, much younger. 'I'd like that.'

'Don't forget to take this file.'

Shirley tucked it securely under one arm. 'Thank you for looking after it. Thank you for helping my father.'

'Don't thank me. I couldn't have done anything else. I wish I could have done more.'

The younger woman reached into her large shoulder bag and pulled out a book. 'Here . . . you might want to read this,' she said. 'Then maybe what I've said will make more sense.' She grimaced. 'It might tell you more than you want to know.'

Megan took the book. 'Take care, dear,' she said. 'And good luck to you.'

'Good luck to all of us.'

When she had gone, Megan looked at the book Shirley had given her. It was by one Dr Rosalie Bertell, titled *No Immediate Danger: Prognosis for a Radioactive Earth*. It was a hefty volume and didn't look as if it would provide a pleasant read. But she knew she would read it.

# Chapter Fourteen

'I don't know how I'll stay awake long enough to cook a meal,' said Megan with a groan, getting out of the taxi.

'You go on up to bed, love,' said Ted. 'You need your rest – I'll fry up something.'

'Don't be daft,' said Megan. 'And don't treat me like I'm about to break. I wouldn't be back at work unless both Dr Baldwin and Baz had said I was fit. I think I can manage to cook – ' She broke off in astonishment, because as Ted opened the door, delicious smells of coffee and frying bacon wafted out.

Anabel was setting the table around Tom who was sitting, either half-asleep or half-stoned, staring at a bowl of dry cornflakes as if he couldn't remember what to do with it. Dave was busy at the cooker.

'Perfect timing,' said Dave. 'The toast is just ready, your eggs will be done in another minute. Sit down, sit down. Anabel has made fresh orange juice.'

Feeling bewildered – but pleasantly so – Megan took her seat. 'To what do we owe this pleasure?' she asked. 'You don't think your mum's too weak to cope with the chores, do you?'

'Not at all. I need the practice,' said Dave. 'We'll be eating in a lot more – we want to save money.'

'I'll do my share, too,' Anabel said hastily. 'I won't make Dave do all the cooking.'

'Good,' said Megan. 'Very admirable. But why the sudden interest in saving money?'

'We want to get our own place,' said Dave. 'We're going to get married.'

Megan's jaw dropped. She looked at Anabel.

'After I get my degree,' said Anabel. 'Not until August or September, at the earliest.'

'Congratulations,' said Ted.

Megan found herself at a loss for words. 'I don't know what to say,' she said. 'I'm very happy.' She burst into tears.

Anabel put her arm around Megan. 'Oh, Megan, you don't mind, do you?'

'I'm happy,' Megan insisted through her tears. 'I'm happy for you, truly . . . truly I am . . . only I'm going to miss our Dave.'

Dave abandoned his cooking to go to his mother. He stroked her hair. 'Come on, Mum,' he said. 'I won't be far away. You'll still see a lot of me. You won't be losing a son – you'll be gaining a daughter.'

By now, Megan's tears had stopped. She sniffed loudly, and wiped her eyes with a paper napkin. 'That's a catchy slogan,' she said. 'Did you make that up all by yourself, Dave?'

'It's why I love him' said Anabel. 'Such a brilliant, original mind.'

'And he's right,' said Megan. 'I always wanted a daughter.' She hugged Anabel. 'Welcome to our family.'

There was something bothering Ted. Megan could tell. And she knew, from years of experience, that he was most likely to talk while they were alone together in his car. If Ted would talk anywhere, he would talk in his car. Some of the most important moments of their relationship had taken place in a parked car. It was one place they could always be sure of being unheard by others.

So she said nothing at home, but on the way to work that evening she said, 'What's bothering you?'

Ted concentrated on driving for a moment, but when he had to stop for a red light he said, 'You.'

'Me? What have I done?'

'I worry about you,' he said uneasily. 'I can't help it. No, don't tell me you're all right! You're not. You're still weak.'

'That's right. I'm not as strong as I was before. It will take time to heal. But that's normal, Ted. I am getting better. It's nothing to worry about.'

'Should you have gone back to work so soon?' he asked. 'Are you sure you were ready?'

'It wasn't only me who was sure – even the doctor said –'

'Never mind the doctor; I want to know about you.' He frowned and gripped the steering-wheel more tightly. 'You didn't *have* to go back to work you know.'

'What do you mean?'

'I mean we could manage on what I make. And Bernard can contribute a bit more, if he gets this job he goes after. You don't have to work. We could manage.'

'We could manage,' said Megan slowly. 'But I'm not sure I could.' She shook her head. 'I need work, Ted. I need to be . . . useful.'

'We need you.'

Megan smiled. '*You* need me. But not every minute of the day. The boys . . . well, they need me less and less. It was different when they were younger, of course, but now they've got their own lives, more and more all the time. Soon Dave will be moving out, starting his own family. We'll probably have Bernard at home a good few years yet, but I think our Tom is getting restless. Looking after them, and the dogs, and the house, isn't enough for me, Ted. I wasn't made to be a lady of leisure. I could always use a few more hours in the day, but I don't want to give up outside work. Not as long as there's a need for what I can do. And there *is* a need. You understand that, don't you Ted?'

'Yeah.'

They had reached Holby City Hospital, but Megan

194

saw by her watch that she still had ten minutes before her shift began. And she didn't think Ted had said all that he had to say. So when he stopped the car she made no move to get out. She simply waited.

'And this job,' he said. 'Working here is special to you, isn't it? It's more important than just any nursing job.'

Megan thought about it. 'Yes,' she said at last. 'I don't mean I couldn't be happy doing something else, and I've liked some jobs more than others, but this one *is* special. It's feeling part of a team. I like that. I like the people I work with – they've become my second family, in a funny sort of way. I think being ill, and being away for a while, and how they responded to it, made me especially aware of how much like a family we all are. We have our quarrels and our disagreements, but basically we care about each other, and we like working together.' She looked at him and frowned. Something was wrong. 'What is it?' she asked. 'What is all this about, Ted, really?'

'You're not going to like it.' Ted sighed heavily. 'It's – oh, hell, maybe it's nothing; maybe they didn't know anything; maybe they were talking off the tops of their heads.'

'*Who*? Ted, what are you talking about?'

'Fare I picked up yesterday,' he said. 'Two blokes, well-dressed. Coming back from some meeting, and talking about how it had gone. The decision that had been made, to close down the casualty unit at Holby City Hospital. Cuts. Inefficient use of funds . . . same old story.'

'Are you sure they were talking about us?'

'I'm sure. One of them even referred to it as being the end of "Plimmer's Army".'

'Oh, my God,' said Megan. She was silent, staggered by the enormity of it. They had talked about this in the department for months – they had been waiting for the axe to fall. It shouldn't have been a surprise, but somehow she had kept hoping that the end would never come. Then she turned on her husband. 'Why didn't you tell me?'

'What d'you mean? I just did!'

'But why wait until now?'

'When should I have told you – when I picked you up this morning? When you looked like you were about to collapse?'

She was silent. Of course he was right.

'Maybe they were wrong,' said Ted. 'Maybe it was nothing, maybe just speculation. There've been rumours before.'

Megan nodded, without conviction. 'I wonder if Ewart has heard.' She heaved a sigh. 'I'd best go in and tell him.'

'I'm sorry, love.'

'So am I,' she said. 'So am I. Let's hope it wasn't true.

*

But it was true. Megan knew that for a fact as soon as she told Ewart what Ted had overheard, and saw his utter lack of surprise. He had already been informed, and was simply waiting for the best moment to break it to the rest of them. Before the end of the shift the entire unit knew the bad news, and were in agreement not to go down without a fight. But how to fight?

The first war-council was held at Megan's house the next evening, before the night shift.

Charlie was the first to arrive, his rickety car packed to the roof with other members of the staff. Although she said nothing about it, Megan noticed that, despite having her own car, Baz had come with Charlie. There had been a great deal of tension between Baz and the head nurse lately, but now both looked happy and relaxed. They had come to some sort of understanding, and settled their differences, but Megan would have been willing to bet that this happy state of affairs could not last. There had always been a powerful attraction between the two, but they were fundamentally too much at odds to succeed as partners. Two headstrong characters, neither willing to give an inch unless it was to his or her own advantage, thought Megan.

'Coffee or tea?' asked Megan.

'Just because we've taken over your house doesn't mean you have to play hostess,' said Charlie. 'I'll make the coffee – you go and sit down.'

Megan would have protested, but when Baz offered Charlie her help, Megan decided to leave the two of them alone together. In any case, the doorbell was ringing, and she had to let the latest arrivals in.

Before long, Megan's sitting-room was packed. Every available space was taken. Susie and Duffy were forced to squash together in one small chair, while another young nurse, Kath Mitchell, perched, looking both pleased and self-conscious, on King's lap. Oliver, always such a sociable dog, had to be forcibly removed from the room. There was no space for anyone who wasn't taking an active part in the business.

Ewart stood in the centre and rapped sharply on a table. The energetic buzz of conversation died away.

'First,' said Ewart, 'I want to thank you all for coming.' He glanced around the room. 'Is everyone here?'

'Kuba's still missing,' said Megan.

'Anyone know the whereabouts of Kuba?'

'He's heading east with Nurse Clemonds,' said Ponting.

'How the young do live,' drawled King.

Laughter filled the room.

Ewart banged on the table. 'Please!'

After a few chuckles and throat-clearings, silence settled on the room again.

'Right,' said Ewart. 'I hardly need to say it, but we've called this meeting to discuss any action we

198

can informally take to protest against the impending closure of our unit.'

'Stop work,' said Charlie.

Megan sat ramrod-straight in her chair. Across the room, Duffy mirrored her posture. 'Charlie,' said Megan, her voice distinctly cool, 'You know the RCN's clause as well as anybody. That is not an option.'

'Join NUPE, then,' said Charlie. 'They'd support a strike if it came to that.'

'That's not the point!'

'Megan, Charlie,' said Ewart earnestly, 'I'm counting on the RCN, NUPE and the BMA all making official noises.'

'That'll be as effective as a dumb guard dog!' said Charlie.

There were murmurs around the room, some agreeing with Charlie, some disapproving.

'What about the patients signing a petition?' suggested Ponting.

Charlie shook his head. 'They don't care that much. Anyway, we haven't got the numbers.'

'They're jolly glad to see us when they're hurt!' said Sandra Mute.

'Precisely.'

'Ewart, we're not going to get very far if everything other than all-out war is automatically written off by Charlie,' King said.

Charlie moved in his seat, about to object. Megan

cut him off, speaking quietly and firmly. 'I'm sorry, but we cannot strike.'

Her voice and manner commanded attention. Everyone looked at her. She went on, slowly, 'To my mind it's a matter of honour.'

Charlie slumped down in his chair, his whole body signalling his anger.

'I'm afraid there are other things to remember,' Ewart said gently. 'One, the permanent night shift was an experiment. They don't have to give us the same notice as they do other wards. Two, they've been very clever. You're not going to lose your jobs – you just get transferred.'

'Where to?' asked King. 'Psycho-geriatrics?'

Ewart ploughed on. 'So, as you see, no union has much of a leg to fight from.'

'But what about the department?' demanded Duffy.

'Every night I see them come in,' Susie said, at almost the same time. 'Where are those patients going to go?'

'Just means we'll have them in the wagon for ten minutes more,' said Mute. 'More, in the rush hour . . . it could kill people, this.'

Everyone was silent. Then, from Ponting: 'I'd say they've got you over a barrel with no hope of a prayer.'

Charlie leaned forward, fists on his knees. 'This is a waste of bloody time! Listen, what we do is, we stop work, sod whichever union we belong to, just show them how much we're needed!'

Duffy and Megan spoke at once from their opposite ends of the room, Megan quietly, Duffy shouting. 'No!'

'Wonderful!' said Charlie. 'So, we work on like heroes and lose the night shift and not a word is said. You tell that to the next RTA who comes in peppered with glass . . .'

'That's exactly who I'm thinking of!' said Megan. 'We get an RTA when we're on strike – what happens then? How is that any different from –'

'I'm talking long-term care!'

'And I – I'm sorry, but I can't do that. I can only care as far as the next poor sod who needs our skills, and I go on working right up till the moment they close those doors.'

Charlie sneered at Megan. 'Very moving.'

'Charlie! There are alternatives to a strike,' said Ewart. 'We can lobby, talk to the press.'

'They're all with BUPA.'

'BUPA doesn't provide casualty services!'

Under, over, and around Ewart and Charlie, people were beginning to talk out of turn. Ewart held up his hands in a plea for order. 'Before you tear each other to pieces, please remember one thing. We've got to move *fast*. They aren't going to give us time to get our act together. There's a new General Manager, and he's using us to make his mark.'

Charlie sighed noisily. 'Look, I'm not trying to stir things but I want to know from the doctors in this room,' he looked pointedly first at Ewart and then, holding eye-contact, at Baz, 'how far would you go to support the nurses if it came to the crunch?'

'Charlie,' said Ewart. 'That's divisive.'

'Baz?'

Baz looked straight back at Charlie. 'We need support,' she said. 'People don't know what we do. They don't realize, unless they're unlucky enough to need us some night. The community only knows what we do when they're affected. You look at the support for the maternity hospital. Everybody knows about children – everybody cares. We've got to make them care that much about us.'

'So?' said Charlie, pressing.

Baz nodded. 'Charlie's right,' she said to the room at large. 'We have to stop work.'

'No!' cried Megan.

'They'll only replace you with another doctor,' said Ponting.

Baz shrugged 'Then we make a lot of noise about it.'

'I'm sorry,' said Megan. She was trembling, but unaware of it. 'I'm sorry, but no! I'll stand outside that department all the hours God gives me telling people that they're closing us down. Damn it. I'll go to the House of Commons. But we cannot, must not, *cannot* strike!'

Charlie stared at Megan, his lips so thin with anger they had gone white. He lurched to his feet, his hands clenching and unclenching at his sides. He looked as if he wanted to hit her. Instead, he strode across the crowded room and out of the door, slamming it hard.

'Excuse me,' said King, and pushing Kath gently but firmly off his lap, he went after Charlie.

'People,' said Ewart wearily. 'People, we are tearing each other to pieces.'

'Correction,' said Ponting. 'The government's tearing you to pieces. And if I was you lot, I'd listen to Charlie.'

Megan was shaking with repressed sobs. When Ewart came and crouched beside her chair, putting his arm around her, she gave up the struggle and wept openly.

The meeting was over, in turmoil and disarray. People left in twos and threes.

Megan blew her nose noisily. 'I love that stupid idiot like a brother!'

'You're tired,' said Ewart helplessly. 'You're not really well yet.'

Megan shrugged wearily. 'Second childhood, more like. Every little thing has me in tears these days. But, oh, Ewart, the way he looked at me . . . as if I . . . it's a matter of principle. He should know that.'

'Of course he knows.'

'If he had the least idea how much I look up to him. Why was I fighting with him? Who closes people like us down? I should be screaming at them, not Charlie.'

'Do you want to take the night off?'

'What? No, of course not. I'm coming in.' She looked around. 'Where's Ted?'

Ted appeared at the sound of his name. He had been hanging back, but was ready when his wife needed him.

Megan stood up, moving away from Ewart, and busied herself tidying up, striving for normality again.

'Give us a hand with the mugs, would you love?' she said to Ted. She glanced at Ewart. 'I'll see you at work in about an hour.'

Ewart shrugged helplessly, then nodded and left. Megan could hear the sound of voices outside, fading into the distance; the noise of cars starting up and driving off. She looked around the cluttered sitting-room, trying to see what had to be done, but once again tears blurred her vision, and she could not move.

Ted, unaware, was gathering up mugs and ashtrays. 'There's lots of things can be done,' Ted said. 'To make people sit up and take notice. I was thinking – we could do a convoy. Seen it on TV. Straight to Downing Street. Every nurse gets a free lift in a taxi. If we did it smart enough we'd get national attention, be on the evening news and the front page of all the papers.'

He looked around for her response. 'You could hand the Prime Minister a letter –' He broke off, seeing that his wife was in tears.

With a pleading look, Megan stretched out her arms towards him like a little girl. Ted went to her and held her tightly. She could feel his heart beating strongly against hers. Gradually, the warmth of him, and his silent, solid strength, calmed her, and she regained control of herself.

'I know he's right,' she said. 'I know there's got to be something . . . I *know*. I don't want to stand aside and do nothing and let them close down the department. But I can't do something I don't believe in; I just can't. And I don't think Charlie should try to make us; that's just as bad. If we go on strike – if the nurses strike, I mean really close the department – God, no one else could do our job – and what about the patients? What would they think? They couldn't trust us anymore.' She pulled away from Ted slightly. 'They've got to be able to trust us.'

Still holding her, now at arm's length, Ted slowly shook his head. 'I'm sorry, girl,' he said. 'I've got to say it. You have to live in the real world.' She stiffened.

'Now, wait,' he said. 'Before you start telling me I'm wrong, you hear me out. Charlie, Baz, Susie, Clive . . . you're all good people, all of you, but not so special. You're no different from thousands of other hospital departments all over the country.'

'I know.'

'No, you don't. At least, you don't believe it. None of you can see beyond the end of your own shift.' He sounded disapproving, but now he looked at her more tenderly. 'So you end up fighting each other when you should be working together, fighting together on the same side. It's not a personal, private problem- it's national. *Every* hospital in the country. *National* Health. *That's* what you're fighting for.'

# Chapter Fifteen

'Hey, Megan,' Susie called from reception as Megan came in to work. She beckoned her over to the desk. 'Duffy and me are going to stick around after work, want to join us?'

Megan hesitated.

'We're not stopping work,' Duffy assured her. 'It's on our own time. I've already told Ewart, and he's going to alert the press.'

Megan smiled. 'Of course I will, but do you really think the press will be interested in what three nurses do in their spare time?'

Susie wrinkled her nose. 'It'll be more than three. Lots more. We're spreading the word around, and getting a good response. Any spare time we've got, we're painting banners. Kuba's got the sheets and paints and stuff for us. And I think we can make it interesting. Give them something to photograph. Remember when we picketed that cinema?'

'Nurses Say No to Naughtiness,' said Megan, remembering the journalistic response.

'That was just one paper, and anyway, this is –'

At that moment Duffy, heavily laden, collided

with a patient's inconveniently-placed rucksack, spilling boxes all over the floor.

The waiting patients looked on with mild interest. 'Don't all rush to help,' Megan said sarcastically, going to lend a hand.

The man whose rucksack it was – a wiry, deeply-tanned and sober-looking individual – was mortified by the trouble he had caused. 'Terribly sorry – all my fault – dreadfully sorry –' he muttered, colliding with Duffy again and again as he tried to help her.

'You planning to camp here?' asked Duffy.

He looked baffled, obviously not recognizing that it was a joke. 'Er, no,' he said.

'Where'd you get the tan?' asked Megan.

'Nigeria.' Suddenly a spasm of discomfort crossed the man's face. He clutched his gut. 'Please, er, excuse me, could you tell me where –'

'Second on your left,' said Duffy, pointing down the corridor.

'Thank you,' he said, 'Thank you so much.' Still with a polite smile, despite his obvious distress, he moved away rapidly in the direction Duffy had indicated.

Megan was amused and rather charmed by the way he clung to the proprieties. 'Last of the Empire,' she said.

'He said Nigeria,' Duffy pointed out.

'So?'

'What's that got to do with Empire?'

'Ah, forget it,' Megan said, smiling. She went away to find the man's card. Brian Finch, his name was. Back from Nigeria, where he had been doing missionary work, about three weeks. Suffering from diarrhoea, stomach pains and fever. As soon as she saw him emerge from the toilet, she called his name, and took him to a cubicle to await a doctor's attention. He was just another patient – and far easier to deal with than a lot of the drunks and loonies who staggered through the doors of the casualty department every night of the year – and it didn't occur to Megan that there was anything special to worry about until she saw Baz's response, and heard her say quietly, 'I want Ewart to take a look.'

'Do you think it's –'

'I don't know,' Baz said, cutting her off. 'Yet. Check how many patients we've got waiting. And hold them.'

Nigeria, thought Megan, going to tell Susie. What was it about Nigeria? There was something at the back of her mind, but she couldn't quite remember it.

When she returned, she found Baz in consultation with Ewart in the corridor, a curtain hiding Mr Finch from view.

'I want to go over his symptoms again,' Ewart was saying. 'It could be anything from flu to glandular fever.'

'We've got pyrexia of unknown origin and a high

risk area,' Baz said in a low, concerned voice.

'Eight waiting,' said Megan.

Ewart shook his head. 'If he's got what you think he's got we're going to have to close shop.'

Baz laughed quietly.

Megan frowned. 'What's funny?'

'I was just thinking, he's about to do what a hundred bureaucrats have been trying to do for the last three months.'

Ewart looked blank. 'Sorry?'

Megan understood. 'Close us down,' she said to Ewart as she walked away. She had just remembered what it was about Nigeria, and she felt as worried now as Baz and Ewart both looked.

Lassa fever.

Megan remembered the first big scare about Lassa fever – when was it, in the seventies? She didn't remember details; only that it was very, very contagious, and people died of it – mostly nurses, doctors, and other patients who had come in contact with the original victim. If there was a chance this man had Lassa fever, they would have to act quickly. They couldn't take risks; they would have to go into quarantine at once, even if it proved afterwards to have been an unnecessary precaution. Far better to look like fools than to be dead.

Ewart reached the same conclusion. Within minutes orders had gone out to the staff. Patients waiting in reception were to be moved into the lobby. No one else was to be admitted. Casualty ward was to be sealed off, the risk of infection contained as much as possible.

'The most important is the number of contacts,' Ewart said to Baz and Megan. 'We need to contain those as soon as possible.'

'I'll phone the Medical Registrar,' said Baz, moving to the telephone.

'Dr Davis?'

Baz nodded.

'Forget it. He wouldn't know a tropical virus if it blew his nose for him.'

'That could be dangerous,' said Baz, putting the phone down.

'Somewhere in this dump of a building is a box with special suits for tropical diseases.'

'What do you do,' asked Baz. 'Die in them?'

'They're for the medical staff! Guards against infection.'

'Bagsy the smallest,' said Baz. 'In red, if there's a choice.'

'This is serious, Dr Samuels,' said Ewart in a voice that struggled, without conviction, for firmness. 'From now on, only you, me and Charlie go near him. OK?'

Baz saluted smartly and marched off.

'I've already been exposed to him and Charlie hasn't,' Megan said. 'Wouldn't it be better –'

At that moment Duffy came racing up, looking

horrified. 'I bumped into his rucksack, and we knelt down and he helped me pick up the boxes. I was as close to him as – as Megan! Wasn't I, Megan?'

Calmly Ewart replied, 'A, we don't know whether he actually has Lassa fever and B, you'll have your temperature checked for the next two weeks.'

Slowly the fear went out of Duffy's face, and she grinned with relief.

'Get a couple of helpers and strip the Plaster Room,' Ewart said. 'Just leave a trolley and a chair. Clear as you can. Who's doing reception?'

'Charlie and Clive. Have you done this before?'

'Tropical diseases? Sort of a hobby.'

'Like fish?'

'Not really, no.'

'No,' said Duffy, nodding. 'Oh, well.' She, too, saluted before she went off to prepare the Plaster Room.

'And that's why they call us Plimmer's Army,' said Megan.

'Check the cubicles and report to Charlie,' said Ewart.

She saluted.

He saluted back.


'Report to Charlie,' Ewart had said. That was going to be awkward; they hadn't so much as exchanged a glance since he had stormed out of her house earlier in the day, and Megan's feelings were still bruised.

She hoped Charlie would make the first move; at least give her some sign that he felt as bad as she did about their disagreement.

She found him in the administration area, rubbing out names on the blackboard. He gave her a sideways glance, but no greeting.

'Fractured metatarsal in six,' Megan said rather stiffly. 'That's all.'

He didn't look at her. 'We got any ambulances outside?'

'One, yes.'

'Warn the driver and hold him till the CP says it's OK to go. We'll need his destination and his address for monitoring.'

Megan nodded, but didn't move. She hated grudges and sulking. 'Don't let the sun go down on your anger,' her mother had always said about family quarrels. Angry words would be spoken, but soon apologized for, soon forgiven and forgotten. She wanted to say something, but she didn't know what. He wasn't making it any easier. She couldn't talk to his back.

Suddenly he turned and gave her a hard, cold look. 'All right?'

Megan nodded, and left. Of course it wasn't all right, but now was not the time to say so.

Kuba found the box of special suits in the cupboard where they had been placed, and nearly forgotten about, more than a decade earlier.

Baz greeted the sight of the first suit with a shriek of disbelief.

'They're like something from outer space!'

'Wait till you see the masks,' said Charlie, pulling the voluminous garment on over his clothes.

'I quite fancy it,' said Duffy. 'Except for the colour . . . one size fits all, OK, but they ought to give you some choice in the colour.'

'Nip in the waist,' said Susie, 'Put some ties at wrists and ankles, fancy it up with a few beads and chains, and ditch the boots, definitely ditch the boots.'

Charlie, the first to be suited up, complete with mask, visor and boots, began to pose. 'How do I look?'

Baz took a good look at him and cracked up.

'Beam me up, Scotty!' King exclaimed.

'Forward, into the past!' cried Baz.

'To boldly go . . .'

They were all laughing now, almost hysterical, except for Ewart.

'Can we start behaving like doctors and nurses, please! This is a very dangerous virus!'

'Not as dangerous as us!' said Duffy.

'They'll never come near us in these,' said Baz. 'Makes a girl feel really safe, this does . . .'

Charlie sat down on the floor, utterly helpless with mirth, and the sight of him made them all laugh harder.

'What's wrong?' Ewart demanded. 'What's wrong with it?'

Megan patted him on his suited shoulder. 'Nothing,' she said, through her laughter. 'Honestly, nothing.'

Mr Finch emerged from the toilet. 'Did you call me?' he asked.

Their laughter froze.

Beyond the double glass doors, in the lobby, the waiting patients applauded this strange tableau.

Then Ewart spoke, bringing his army back to earth and smartly to attention. 'Right! Let's go. Get that loo sealed off. And all the rest of the doors. Now!'

They worked together swiftly and efficiently. Somehow, the bout of silliness had revived them, working like a tonic on frayed nerves, weary bodies and stretched tempers. And having laughed together made it impossible to go on bearing a grudge.

Charlie and Megan found themselves briefly alone in a corridor, and looked at each other.

'Charlie,' said Megan tentatively. 'About the meeting –'

'I was rude,' he said. 'I'm sorry. I lost my temper and I shouldn't have – at least, I shouldn't have lost it at you. We want the same thing, even if we don't agree on the best way, we shouldn't be fighting each other.'

'That's what Ted said. He said it's not just about

us, and not just this hospital, but everyone – we can go on fighting for our little department, but it's a bigger fight than that. The changes have to be made nationally.

'He's right, your Ted.'

'Oh, Charlie, I –'

'Now, now,' he said, holding up an admonishing finger. 'Don't go getting soppy!'

Megan grinned. He smiled back. She put her arms around him and gave him a good, strong hug.

'Remind me never to arm-wrestle with you,' said Charlie when they separated.

'Charlie,' Megan said. 'I don't know if you've heard, but we're having a bit of a demo as soon as the shift is over. Duffy and Susie have been organizing . . .'

He was shaking his head.

'Oh, Charlie, why not?'

'Because it won't do any good.'

'How do you know it won't? At least it's something – get some attention, a few minutes on the lunch-time news – something to let people know we're here. How can it hurt? Tell me that?'

'It's like putting a plaster on a sucking chest wound,' Charlie said. 'Not only does it not do any good, it gives people a false sense of accomplishment.'

'But –' with difficulty, Megan mastered her rising anger. She managed to keep her voice even as she said, 'You mean, a strike or nothing?'

'Yes.' He looked at her, and held up a hand to forestall argument. 'I know . . . I know how you feel about that. You have your principles, believe me, I have principles, too.'

'We're on the same side, Charlie.'

'I know that. We're wearing the same uniform.' He made a sweeping gesture to indicate their bulky suits. Megan laughed.

'Truce,' she said.

'Truce.'

The Community Physician was Dr Gould, a middle-aged lady with an enormous beehive hairdo and large, diamante-studded spectacles. She arrived as Duffy and King were applying chlorhexadrene on everything Finch might have touched. She was impressed by the speed and thoroughness with which precautions had been taken, and said so to Ewart Plimmer before asking for an isolation vehicle or ambulance to be made ready to take Mr Finch away.

The telephone rang. Ewart picked it up. 'Casualty. No, we're closed. Still disinfecting. A few hours, at least.' He hung up.

Watching him, Megan wondered how many people their temporary closure would affect. Probably not very many. How many people would even notice? Again, not many. Only those few who might have had need of their services tonight, and those few people weren't going to keep the unit open now that the management had decided to shut it down. A strike, whether it was for days or weeks, would have no greater effect than this one night's unintentional strike, she thought, and it could only hurt people. Why didn't Charlie see that? She headed for the staffroom to join the other nurses for a cup of tea, and to wait for the end of the shift.

When at last the long night was over, and the morning shift arrived to find an unusually clean and empty ward, Megan went out to the ambulance bay with Clive, Kuba, Duffy and Susie. She caught sight of Ted's taxi, and began to smile. Taped to the side was a home-made banner bearing the words 'Save Casualty'.

For once, instead of waiting in the car, Ted got out, leaving it parked in front of a prominent 'No Standing' sign, and came to meet Megan, giving her a kiss and a big hug.

'I like the new decoration,' she said.

'All the other lads have them as well,' he said. 'The whole city will know about it before the end of the day!'

The sound of cheering, and singing, floated on the early morning air. Megan and Ted turned and looked up at the hospital.

From every window in the large building sheets, banners, flags, or rolls of paper now unfurled.